THE LIBERTY WARS

BOOK ONE

CLARK RAYDER

ISBN-13: 979-8-218-07830-0

Library of Congress Control Number: 2022917700
Cover design by: Clark Rayder
Printed in the United States of America

Dedicated to my wife, Alice Rayder. Without your help and guidance, this would never have been possible.

CHAPTER 1

A low-hanging sun was falling into the horizon of an infinite desert, radiating its nomadic sky with a deep orange. This desolate realm was known as the Southern Wastes, and in another world and in another time, it would have been the lower deserts of California.

Along one of the many jagged dirt highways that ran through the boundless domain, a convoy of three timeworn box trucks made their way deeper into the forbidden expanse. The vehicles looked as if they were native to the land—tattered, sandblasted, and better left behind if not for their utility in such a place.

Watching the ragged convoy from an elevated distance, less than a mile away, was Arlo Shaw and his fellow soldier, Lambert Ashcroft. Both men were weathered veterans of the British Empire's never-ending global military conquest, which as of late was unleashed upon the American cause and its viral philosophy. The third member of their group was Lambert's purebred Dutch Shepard, Lucy, who was seated beside the men with a heavy pant and drooping tongue.

After lowering his dirt-covered binoculars, Arlo spoke with a commanding voice, one that made him the incontestable leader. "Three trucks, twelve-man team . . ."

"Sounds like a match," replied Lambert with a jaded stoicism that was uniquely his.

"You ready?" Arlo asked.

"I've waited ten years for this day."

Arlo gave his friend a familiar smile, saying, "I assume you've already started looking for places?"

"I've already drawn the property line."

"I know I've asked you before, but why a cattle ranch? After everything we've seen and done together. That's what you want?"

"Why politics? If we've learned anything in our time together, it's that it doesn't work."

"It doesn't work because of those who work in it."

"And you still think you're going to change that?"

"I'm sure as hell going to try."

Upon Arlo's answer, Lambert scoffed and said,

"The King will never allow anything to change. He only listens to the think tanks and to the wankers who kiss his arse."

"Well, for the sake of your retirement plan, I would suggest considering some optimism," Arlo said, as he slung his camouflaged rifle around himself, securing it with an aggressive pull on the retention strap.

Lambert knew from Arlo's familiar tone that neither man was going to convince the other of his view, and to make the point of it, he turned away and descended the gravel path of the hill with Lucy. After several steps, he told Arlo, "Well, when the world fails you, you know where to find me. . . . " Arlo replied with nothing but a confident smile as he left the rock ledge and followed close behind.

From head to toe, Arlo and Lambert were dressed in desert camouflage patterns that kept them well concealed amidst the matching terrain. There was an overused quality to their equipment that suggested it was trusted to endure the trials of their long and inspiring careers as operators in the Crown's elite special forces.

After coming down the hill and emerging from behind the rock walls, both men came upon the remaining members of their task force, Gale Robinson and Bohden Brooks. At the sight of Arlo, Bohden composed himself and shook off his relaxed posture. In a gravelly Scottish voice, he asked, "Well? Tell me we didn't come out here for nothin'."

"No. We're green. Ready up," replied Arlo with momentum as he joined the others. Arlo's words prompted Gale to rise from his run-ragged four-wheeler, one of two that were present. As he casually rested his high-powered sniper rifle across his chest, he inquired of Arlo with a silent strength and a calculated voice, "Any changes, or we sticking to the plan?"

"No need to complicate things yet. We'll keep it as is. But just remember, we bring him in alive. He's no good to anyone dead," Arlo replied.

"Right. We fuck that up and they'll make us do another ten years," said Bohden, to which Lambert promptly stated, "Let 'em try."

Arlo was quick to redirect. "I get it, we're all nervous, but today is no different from any other."

"But tomorrow is. . . ." asserted Lambert.

"He's right, chief. Not even one of your bloody speeches is gonna change my mind this time," said

Bohden.

A grin formed on Arlo's face; the friendly expression then became an optimistic smile as he rallied his men for the last time he would ever need to. "For King and Country, then," he said, invoking the mantra of the British Empire.

Promptly, Gale and Bohden echoed, "For King and Country."

"Alright, that's enough," said Lambert as he interrupted his partner and pulled him from the meeting. "Let's just get this over with. Gale, signal us when you're in position."

"Copy that," Gale replied as he corralled Bohden back to the ATVs. Both men promptly secured their loose items to the racks and then saddled the desert runners. They each kicked the ignition until the stubborn motors turned over. With a slight turn of the throttle, they accelerated forward and drove away, leaving thick plumes of dry dust amidst the rumbling coughs of the ornery engines.

As the other team members departed, Arlo and Lambert approached an overused heavy hauler truck that was parked in the shallow shade of the rock wall, well hidden from view. The vehicle's eroded texture and timeworn surface matched its surroundings like a chameleon.

When Lambert pulled down the rusted tailgate, Arlo couldn't help but notice his partner's quiet tone and focused eyes. Arlo knew that Lambert was wrestling with his intuition, which was often provoked by suspicion. "Somethin' on your mind?" Arlo asked.

"It's all too smooth. Target's on time. We're ahead of schedule. Everything's in position. Even intel managed to get us everything we needed. Tell me when that's ever happened."

"So, what's the problem?"

"There isn't one, which means it's coming. . . ."

Arlo shook his head. "Last-op jitters, that's all it is."

"Let's hope," replied Lambert, who then pressed his tongue to his teeth, and sounded a commanding whistle that directed Lucy to follow him into the truck.

·   ·   ·

In the crosshairs of Gale's precision rifle scope, the target convoy slowed their progress and came to a stop within an open clearing bordered by small rocky hills layered with sand and dirt. Before the dust settled, the occupants of the vehicles exited and walked with militant posture to establish a perimeter around the convoy.

What Gale and Bohden observed from their position were soldiers of a different order. They were, like all American fighters, visibly under-funded and ragged in appearance. They were desperate and derelict compared to the distinguished and superior Empire that opposed them.

One by one, Gale and Bohden began their search of the American personnel, stopping and studying each face through the aided view of their advanced optics.

"Do you see him?" asked Bohden with a worried voice.

"Patience . . ." Gale urged as he continued his machine-like scan of the Americans, passing from one magnified face to the next.

After his first scan yielded nothing, Gale turned his fraying ball cap backwards and stiffened up. After adjusting for the rising anxiety, Gale doubled back his search, but there was still no sign.

"I swear if intel fucked us again . . ." said Bohden.

"He's here, he's gotta be. He can't afford to pass— There! Middle truck, passenger side," said Gale with certainty.

Bohden abruptly snapped his view in Gale's direction. As he did, his spotter scope became filled with an array of computer graphics, squares, and scanning programs that all magnetized to the face of the man in view.

To validate the target, Bohden initialized a program to cross-reference the man's bellicose face with a military intelligence database of known high-value targets of the Crown. Hundreds of faces were cycled through the program until a match was confirmed with the name Caylen Cross.

Along with Caylen's identification came a rap sheet of information that included his role as a high-ranking asset of the notorious American Underground— more specifically for his involvement in the militant wings of the organization.

To conclude his findings, Bohden grabbed his radio mic, which was affixed to his gear. With a firm press on the call button, he opened a channel to Arlo and told him, "Target in sight, chief."

"Copy, we're inbound," relayed Arlo over the radio.

Like a stalking specter, Gale kept the reticle of his crosshairs on Caylen as he stepped away from his vehicle. Gale was determined to learn all he could in the time he had; and what he saw was that Caylen was a foreboding figure. He was towering, cold, and obscured by an aura of mystery. Gale then toggled his scope's magnification, bringing Caylen's scabrous and impatient face into better view.

"Ugly son of a bitch," said Bohden.

"Don't call the kettle black. . . ."

"What do you mean?"

"Never mind."

Accustomed to Gale's highbrow taunts, Bohden shrugged off the comment and went back to his observations, telling Gale, "Arlo better hurry this up; he looks like he's ready to split."

"When you get to his level, the world runs on your time."

"Was that a compliment?"

"Like any decent adversary, I respect him. That's

not the same as a compliment."

"Aye. Don't call the kettle black."

"That's not how you would use that phrase."

"Whatever."

Before Bohden could find a suitable comeback, the rhythmic pounding of a diesel engine grabbed his and Gale's attention. It was Arlo, arriving just in time to stave off everyone's impatience.

Gale whipped his crosshairs to the nearby rock hill where he saw the vehicle emerge. He followed its slowing pace as it neared Caylen and his men, who were looking at it suspiciously.

"Here we go," said Gale as the truck finally came to a stop.

After fighting the corroded gears, Arlo eventually jammed the truck into park and stepped out. The busted door barely stayed closed, even after being slammed. As Arlo walked ahead, Lucy's eyes became nervous when she lost sight of him. Lambert was quick to notice, causing him to give a quiet order for Lucy to crawl down beneath the dash.

"He'll be fine," Lambert said in a near whisper as he comforted Lucy with a gentle rub between her ears.

To disguise themselves for the meeting, Arlo and Lambert had swapped their military uniforms for the garments of nomadic gunrunners. Both men were covered in dirty and aging rags, which served as protection from the incessant sun. However, based on Caylen's posture, Arlo could tell that it was going to take some convincing to sell the disguise.

Years of training with Crown Intelligence had given Arlo a mental arsenal of tips and tools to read the psychology of his adversaries, and Caylen was a classic stonewaller.

"You look taller in person, Caylen," began Arlo in a confident and sly tone as he tried to instill a sense of familiarity. However, much to Arlo's disappointment, Caylen was unmoved and emotionless. He gave nothing to work with.

Arlo continued by trying to brush it off and improvise before any more doubt could infect the deal. He stepped forward and said, "Is this how you greet all your recruits?"

"That's far enough," replied Caylen with a thick, demanding Irish accent. Arlo stopped himself mid-step, careful to not provoke anything.

Lambert could feel that the pressure of the meeting would not break anytime soon. Unlike Arlo, Lambert trusted his own gut over the Crown's claims of psychology. In a far less diplomatic approach, Lambert read the faces and the movements of Caylen's men, sizing them up for who would move first. His mind then raced through how to handle the worst-case scenario. He envisioned firing a burst of shots through the windshield that would take out the first two or three targets. By then, Gale would have followed up to deal with anyone who could react. There would be a straggler or two but amidst the chaotic onset of gunfire, Lambert could displace to a flanking position and gain back any advantage. Once his support was gone, Caylen would probably try to run, but not fast enough to escape Lucy.

With his thoughts complete, Lambert gripped his sub-machine gun close, ready and willing to act out his tactical script.

Before the meeting could reach the much-feared dissolution, Caylen addressed Arlo with a cryptic phrase, "The stars are numbered . . ."

"And thirteen will lead the way," said Arlo in response to the coded message.

"Who's the tagalong?" Caylen continued.

"That's my brother, Dominick. You said you would take any willing and able man, right?"

"You vouch for him, then?"

"With my life."

"And he has taken the oath?"

"Yes. Same as me."

"Then bring him out."

As Caylen finished, Arlo turned to Lambert and gestured for him to come out from the truck. Lambert knew that if he did not comply, the suspicion would only worsen. He then gently and reluctantly placed his weapon on the seat and gave an inconspicuous signal to Lucy, commanding her to stay and keep quiet.

Lambert stepped out from the truck and took his place beside Arlo. Both men kept their focus on Caylen, who was busy digging through the cargo of the vehicles.

"What did you tell him?" Lambert grunted, with enough caution to avoid suspicious ears and eyes.

"That you're my brother, and that I vouch for you with my life."

"I'm flattered."

"Well, 'least you know half of it is true."

"First time I've heard of it."

"We can do therapy later, just work with me."

"Copy that."

When Caylen returned, he brought with him a worn rifle case that he set at Arlo's feet. "They may not be elegant, but they are reliable," said Caylen.

"Effective is all that matters, right?" Arlo added as he leaned down and zipped open the fraying fabric. Inside, there were two archaic rifles, one of which he grabbed and lifted for inspection. "M-15 Baltic surplus," said Arlo while he studied the grizzled rifle.

Lambert could tell that the knowledge Arlo had for the weapons helped to alleviate Caylen's suspicions. Lambert then strengthened their disguise by soliciting Caylen for information. "You have the coordinates for the delivery?"

"Of course," Caylen replied as he gave Lambert a folded piece of paper from his jacket pocket.

"This is everything?" asked Lambert as he maneuvered his way further into his role.

"Yes, we will need these shipments delivered to those locations by nightfall tomorrow."

"Consider it done," Lambert concluded after quickly glancing through the paper.

"I admire your assurance; it's something that our people have been lacking lately."

"Well, hopefully this is the start of something new," added Arlo with an undertone of optimism.

"My men will help you load the rest," finished Caylen as he lifted his hand and waved for his men to complete the transfer of supplies.

.   .   .

After the exchange was salvaged and finished, Caylen's men departed from the area, leaving Arlo and Lambert to decompress and discuss the aftermath amongst themselves as they packed up.

"Rough start, but altogether I'd say that went rather smooth," claimed Arlo after slamming shut the tail gate of their loaded truck.

"I'm just glad that we're finally done. This kinda shit never sat right with me, anyway. It's bloody entrapment."

"At least fewer people get killed this way."

"For now, but eventually the next generation learns about this kind of shit, and then another bomb goes off. Starts it all over."

Eager to argue Lambert's point, Arlo replied, "That's one way to look at it."

"This should be good. Tell me, what am I missing?"

"There's always the bigger picture. Once we match the weapons, we send in bravo team for the arrest. They bring 'em in, Caylen cuts a deal to give up the bigger players, and eventually we get to the top. The whole thing will come down on itself after that."

"So why hasn't it worked so far? We've been chasing blokes like him since we started. Come to think of it, this mission, our last, looks and feels an awful lot like our first ten years ago. . . . And yet still no bloody Minuteman."

"War is never easy; it's gonna take more work."

"Face it. The man's a ghost, Arlo."

The sound of approaching ATVs caught Arlo's and Lambert's attention. As they turned to trace the sound, they found Gale and Bohden had arrived from beyond the rock hills.

"Don't look so disappointed," said Lambert as he noticed Gale's solemn face.

"He's just upset he lost the bet," replied Bohden, answering for Gale.

"Do I want to know?" Lambert asked.

"Later. We need to scan these rifles," urged Gale, eagerly attempting to change the subject.

As Gale took one of the weathered rifles, he inspected its markings, eventually finding a serial number stamped into the worn steel of the receiver. He then equipped a small handheld computer that he used to make a quick detail scan of the image. Once complete, Gale was able to cross-reference the number with another Imperial database. Once a positive match was indicated by the graphic display, he informed the team, "Confirmed."

Driven by the finding, Arlo grabbed his radio switch and made a transmission. "Bravo, this is Paladin. We have a match on the rifles; you're green to make the grab."

A static-distorted voice abruptly answered, "Negative, Paladin. Orders are to stand down."

Puzzled, Arlo pressed for an answer. "What do

you mean? Orders from who?"

Before there was a response, the thunderous sound of approaching helicopters gave him the answer.

Just beyond the hills, a flight of two Imperial helicopters emerged and made a flyby over Arlo and his team. The low altitude of the military-grade engines shook the surroundings, prompting Arlo to shout, "Fucking Wallcroft!"

.   .   .

Within moments of their arrival, the two Imperial helicopters chased down Caylen's inferior convoy with ease. Once they were within intercept range, one aircraft moved to hold a parallel position to Caylen while the other chased from behind. Captain Octavian Wallcroft, a notorious officer within Crown Intelligence, was in the former of the two.

The calm, collected, and ruthless Imperial officer leaned forward to command his aerial marksman seated on the edge. "Our target is in the passenger seat of the middle vehicle. Kill the rest."

"Understood, sir," replied the faceless Imperial

soldier as he aimed his rifle.

Wallcroft then stepped across the cabin to order his pilot, "Don't let them get any farther! We take them now!"

After the command was given, both helicopters immediately sped up ahead of the convoy and maneuvered with tactical excellence, settling to a hover just above the desert floor. With the passage ahead cut off, Caylen's trucks were forced to come to an abrupt stop.

At the hopeless sight of Imperial air support, Caylen's men began to panic and flee their vehicles. Without hesitation, Wallcroft's soldiers opened fire upon them. One after the other, they fell like frightened deer in a rigged hunt. As the gunfire erupted, Caylen's driver was hit twice through the side window. Dodging the debris of exploding glass and a bursting mist of blood, Caylen leaped for the door, attempting to flee the truck.

Only a few of Caylen's soldiers were able to arm themselves and return fire, but they were swiftly dealt with by the accuracy and precision of the trained Imperial sharpshooters. Once the last of the opposition had fallen, the survivors of Caylen's squadron retreated to the back of the convoy where there was temporary cover.

"What are we supposed to do!?" pleaded one of the Americans, looking to Caylen for leadership. Caylen said nothing. Instead, he walked out from behind cover to meet the Imperials.

As Caylen surrendered himself, Wallcroft's helicopter came down for a landing. The second aircraft responded by moving to a higher altitude, orbiting the area like a patrolling hawk, ready to provide additional force if needed.

Caylen was drained of his patience for what he regarded as the dishonor and schemes of the Empire. He instead sourced the only weapon he had left, which was to be unmoved and jaded. He was compelled to give the Empire nothing but a cold surrender that he believed was far from earned or deserved.

Traversing the short distance, he entered the rotor wash of Wallcroft's helicopter. In doing so, his whole body was blasted with a massive wall of swirling dirt and sand.

Wallcroft's soldiers leaped from the helicopter to apprehend Caylen. Better known as the Imperial Legion, Wallcroft's men were distinguished by their next-generation appearance. Their equipment looked as if it came from a world of tomorrow. It was smooth, unscathed, and dreadfully advanced in comparison to that of Arlo's team.

As the Imperial soldiers rushed toward Caylen, they kept their rifles fixed and aimed. Their voices came from beneath their helmets, which covered their entire heads and faces, and as such their words were amplified and laced with a computer-driven sound. "Down! Get down! Now!" they shouted as they approached Caylen.

"Only if you agree to spare my men!" Caylen said in return, with his eyes locked on Wallcroft, who was walking toward him as if to claim him as a trophy. Caylen continued with his terms. "I will surrender myself willingly and go with you if you spare the lives of these men."

"Do you really think you're in a position to negotiate?" replied Wallcroft as he emerged through the rotor winds with a flowing black obsidian cape.

"It's me you're after, isn't it!? Let them go."

"I have a better idea."

The Imperial soldiers struck Caylen to the ground and bound him with magnetic bindings, the sight of which was enough to convince Caylen's men that they would be next in line. To avoid their inevitable capture, they tried to run but were gunned down by Wallcroft's squadron. No one survived.

As Caylen witnessed the abrupt execution of his men, he raged with streams of concussive blood spewing from his mouth, "You fucking cowards; they were unarmed!"

Wallcroft cared nothing for Caylen's words. He simply ordered, "Grab him."

The soldier nearest to Caylen yanked him up from the ground. He then shoved him forward with the metal stock of his rifle. Just before Caylen was taken aboard the aircraft, Arlo's truck came skidding and sliding onto the scene.

Arlo did not skip a beat. He leaped out with the truck still running. He then gathered himself to command Wallcroft with all the fury and authority his lungs could muster, "Just what the fuck do you think you're doing!? The order was to capture these men, not execute them!" By the time Arlo finished scolding Wallcroft, the gap between them was no more than ten feet.

As he moved to meet Arlo, Wallcroft kept his

words calm and collected, despite his smirking mouth and condescending eyes. "Forgive me, but I fail to see what the problem is."

"Don't think you are going to walk clean from this, you pompous prick."

"I have no such plan to do anything of the sort. On the contrary, I intend to be awarded for disposing of conspirators against the Crown."

"As of this moment, and despite your actions," Arlo replied, "I am still the ranking officer of this operation, and I am giving you an order. That man is leaving here with me, not you."

Wallcroft took several steps forward and leaned into Arlo's face. "Just remember, as soon as you get back, your time in the service of His Majesty will be over . . . and then the task of resolving this pathetic insurrection will fall to me . . . thankfully." Saying nothing more, he turned to walk toward his helicopter. As he arrived, he nodded for his men to release Caylen.

Wallcroft's soldiers removed Caylen's bonds and then shoved him toward Arlo. The soldiers then followed Wallcroft as he stepped into the roaring aircraft. Once boarded, the look on Wallcroft's face promised Arlo a scathing revenge.

With every Imperial aboard, the engines of the helicopter rose in power, causing the rotors to cycle faster and faster. As the swirling blades lifted the chopper off the ground, another storm of dust and debris was propelled across the area until the aircraft joined formation with the other and was gone.

Once the dust settled, Arlo walked toward the wreckage of Caylen's convoy. All he saw was disgrace and misconduct, a formless void absent of humanity.

Once he was close enough, Caylen yanked himself away from Bohden's grip and knelt to mourn a bullet-riddled corpse at his feet. "Where was the honor in this?" asked Caylen. "Wallcroft isn't concerned with honor," replied Lambert, answering for Arlo, who was still in a shock of anger and confusion.

Lambert continued on, pacing the scene with Lucy, who tried to sniff and scout in hopes of a survivor. Finding nothing, Lambert turned to see if Bohden's search yielded something different, "Bohden, you got any survivors?"

Bohden said nothing as he shook his head despondently.

With his nerves at the limit, Arlo turned to give his final order of the day. "Gale, I want photos of everything. The vehicles, the bodies, I want it all."

"Understood," was all Gale said as he reached for his equipment.

"We're wasting our time, Arlo. You know Wallcroft is untouchable," Lambert contested.

"Not this time."

CHAPTER 2

After their extraction from the windswept deserts of the Southern Wastes, Arlo's team had flown through the night to reach the border of an area where the state of Colorado would have been. The team's helicopter flew at a level pace above the expanse of verdant pine as it approached an isolated military base concealed deep within the alpine realm.

As the aircraft came closer, antennae, communication arrays, and blinking landing lights resolved into view. Officially known as Fort Hutchinson, the fort's strategic location served as an ideal central axis for the Crown to conduct its affairs across the troubled continent of the western Imperial Union.

Upon arrival to the fort, the helicopter made a sweeping circular pass around the covert base. From the cockpit, the pilots could see the familiar field of concrete landing pads, where countless other rotor wing aircraft were parked or awaiting take off.

Lining the perimeter of this were many columns of barracks and supply facilities that composed the rest of the fort. From the aerial vantage, it was easy to see the many soldiers and officers as they walked about the base like programmed information traveling through circuits and chipsets. Each of them had their part of the whole to maintain the intricate operation of the special forces black site.

As the helicopter locked in for final approach, a digital display was projected upon the windshield. Once the system was online, an artificially intelligent software guided the pilots in for optimal touchdown. Both pilots used the digital readout to maneuver the aircraft through a holographic tunnel of computer-generated squares calculated by the intelligent system.

Just before the landing was complete, Bohden noticed that Colonel Sheridan, their commanding officer, was outside and eagerly awaiting their arrival. "Look alive, boys, boss is on deck," said Bohden with caution.

"He's never done that before," Gale replied.

Lambert then offered his theory for the Colonel's peculiar posture. "That is what we call damage control."

The weathered landing gear of the helicopter finally touched the ground of Fort Hutchinson. As soon as the aircraft settled into the tarnished concrete, the pilot twisted the collective to lower the power output to the rotor. With the engine throttle now descending, the rotors wound down like slowing fan blades. The rapid sweeps became long, swooping turns that eased the violent winds enough that it was safe for personnel to move about the area.

Arlo was first to leap out onto solid ground. With him came Caylen, whom Arlo held with a tight grip. Following closely behind was the rest of the team, who appeared exhausted and depleted from everything that had transpired. Everyone shared an equal expression of profound injustice over Wallcroft's actions.

As the despondent team arrived to meet Sheridan, a motorcade of raven-black box cars pulled up near the landing site. Their sudden arrival prompted Arlo and his men to take notice, but there was no mystery regarding what was about to occur. Crown Intelligence had arrived to take Caylen into the abyss of interrogation by any means necessary.

Much like the Legion, Crown Intelligence was

gifted with all the next-generation technology the Empire had to offer. This was evident by the polished obsidian masks the group wore as they emerged from the motorcade. The advanced headpieces wrapped around each member's entire face and compounded an already anonymous appearance by hiding both their eyes and expressions.

As Arlo handed his captive over, he saw nothing but his own reflection in the glossy mask of the suited specter before him. No words were exchanged, just an unspoken understanding that Caylen was headed to a place where he may never be seen again.

Once the intelligence teams departed, Arlo and his men motioned to stand at attention for Sheridan, who was an unmovable figure of stone. All emotion had been left behind at some distant threshold in his long career. His expressions and demeanor were always straight to the point, no room for anything but perpetual progress of the Empire.

All four soldiers gave the proud Colonel a formal salute. In response, Sheridan saluted back, telling the team, "Excellent work, gentlemen. I've been told to give you a personal thanks from His Majesty himself."

"The King knows about this?" inquired Arlo with perplexed curiosity.

"Absolutely. We are now officially one step away from the Minuteman."

"Does the King know about Wallcroft, too, then?" said Lambert.

Sheridan was a hard man to move, but Lambert's poignant question drilled right to the core of the thick suspicions that were looming. "I'll see to it that the maneuver goes on his record, but right now we need to focus on what you men have accomplished. This will change the course of the war."

"With all due respect, sir, that wasn't a maneuver . . . it was a massacre," said Arlo.

A silence lingered as Sheridan formed an official response, something he knew would be on record. However, he decided on something more personal. "Is this how you all feel?" he asked.

Bohden was first to answer. "Nothing about how this ended sits right with any of us, sir. I think we're all just left at that."

Arlo then seized the conversation, asking, "If permissible, sir, I would like our own personal notes and account of what happened today to be included in your documentation."

"I'll consider it," replied Sheridan, who then concluded by telling the team, "You gentlemen are relieved."

.   .   .

Lambert and Lucy were the first to arrive through the fabric door of the barracks. As Lambert set foot inside, Lucy ran in front of him and took her place on his disheveled mattress. His tired face then lifted with hope at the sight of something. "I don't believe it," he uttered in an astonished tone.

Waiting for Lambert, as well as every member of Arlo's team, was a sealed envelope with an elegant inscription upon it. The anticipation compelled Lambert to rush forward and tear into the royal document. As he read the letter aloud, the rest of the team entered.

"In recognition of completing ten years of service in His Majesty's Armed Forces, Lambert D. Ashcroft is, by order of the King, eligible for honorable discharge, should he so wish."

" 'Should he so wish'? Can you believe the nerve they have? Who would volunteer to continue conscription?" said Bohden, mocking the Imperial tone of the letter.

"I can think of one or two," replied Gale, eyeing Arlo.

"No, this is it, we're done. We're free men," Lambert attested with a joy he had not known for years.

"Aye. I'll drink to that," said Bohden as he set his gear upon his bed.

Gale, the civil and rational mind of the group, was quick to question the proposal. "Our first night as free men, and you want to get drunk?"

"You heard me right. I haven't tasted a pint since I was twenty-five and tossed aboard that damn bus to Hereford."

"As I remember, the only reason they caught you in the first place was because of all those pints," countered Gale.

"Aye, they did find me in that alley, forged paperwork and all."

Seeking to gather the entire team for the evening, Lambert turned to Arlo, who was the only one who had not said a word. It was clear that Arlo's mind was still lost in the aftermath. Lambert tried to uplift his partner, asking him, "What about you, Arlo? Will you celebrate with us?"

"I'll join you after I finish the report."

Shocked by his words, Bohden told Arlo, "Did you not read the paper, Arlo? We're free, we're done."

"I told you some may volunteer to continue," said Gale under his breath.

Arlo was unmoved. Instead, he gave Bohden a hollow assurance. "You guys go on ahead. I'll see what I can do to join you."

The group could tell Arlo's words were final. There was no shifting him away from the loyalty he had for duty, even if it was no longer an obligation.

.   .   .

Later that day, Arlo was called by Sheridan for a personal debriefing regarding the controversial operation. For some time, he waited in the sterile corridor of the officer's wing, just outside the Colonel's office.

As Arlo looked upon the various golden-framed

portraits of Imperial war heroes that lined the white marble hallway, he reflected upon his time in the service, recalling all the missions and deployments around the world that he believed were all worth it.

Arlo's belief in the causes of the Crown made him conflicted about leaving the military. His ruminations went back and forth countless times as he debated a career in Parliament, or a career as an officer. Both outlets could offer the chance for change from within, which is exactly what he was convinced he could achieve with either avenue.

Before Arlo could find certainty in his thoughts, Sheridan stepped out and took a proud posture. Arlo immediately rose to salute. Sheridan gave one in return, then addressed Arlo in a somber tone. "Let's take a walk."

Sheridan led Arlo outside the building and into the grid-like maze of the base. As they walked, the chatter of procedures and routines at the fort could be heard against Sheridan's curious silence. He wasn't sure where to begin. It was clear his thoughts were elsewhere, so he started with what was most familiar, the mentorship he had built with Arlo. "I understand you're thinking of heading into Parliament?"

"Debating it, sir."

"Good. They could use someone with your experience."

"I hope they'll share your optimism."

"I'll be sure to write them on your behalf."

"You would do that?"

"Absolutely," Sheridan stated confidently, hoping to win Arlo's heart for where he planned to take him. "Our man gave us quite a bit more than we were expecting."

"That's odd. I didn't expect a radical like him to cooperate so fast."

"I don't agree or support what Wallcroft did, but I think it was enough to break the man's hope for the Americans. Seems it made him willing to work with us."

"So, you'll petition for a court martial, then?"

Sheridan stopped mid-step to address Arlo's question. "Wallcroft is Crown Intelligence. With his connections and pull, it'll be months before I can even get a request far enough for consideration. We don't have that kind of time."

"What do you mean? Did something happen?"

"Caylen has given us the location of the Minuteman. The Ministry wants to move on it now, which means they will task Wallcroft and his team to do it. Now, there is the option that I can take command of the operation and convert it to a joint task force between special forces and intelligence. That would provide us the option of the SAS leading the raid, but I am only willing to do that if you and your team delay your discharge for one last mission. I don't have anyone else available that I can trust with this."

"With all due respect, sir, the mission we just came from was supposed to be our last."

"I know what I'm asking of you and your men, but I'll need your response by tonight."

"Tonight!? How fast are they planning to move on this?"

"I've given you all I can. Just trust that they have their reasons. But also know that the Crown can't force you to take this. You've completed your service; anything from this point on is voluntary."

"Is there really no other way? No other option?"

"You know how the world is, Lieutenant. They're tired of this war. It's been losing the support it needs for months now. The politicians want out of it and the people are tired of being taxed for it. I wish things were different, I really do, but if something doesn't change soon, the next option will be the peace treaties from Parliament. The day an American is allowed to sit at the negotiating table is the day that this will have all been for nothing."

"If we bring you the Minuteman, is it enough to end the war?"

"It will be more than enough. You have my word."

.   .   .

The nearest form of civilization to Fort Hutchinson was a small mountain town populated by miners, loggers, and freight drivers passing through the many high-altitude highways of the area. The town itself was only a square-mile patch of land divided down the middle by a main road that hosted an array of humble local businesses. At the heart of the main street was a tavern, which was the only thing keeping the native population afloat. It was here that Lambert, Gale, and Bohden were celebrating their first night as free men.

At the crowded, bustling bar in the center of the tavern, Gale was waiting for an order of drinks. He did his best to ignore the abrasive twangs and rhythms of the blaring folk tunes playing throughout the rustic establishment. Eventually, Gale was served two fresh, bubbling, cold pints of ale. As he gripped the handles of the glasses, they felt icy to the touch.

Ales in hand, Gale made his way through the lively main room that had grown in customers two-fold since his arrival only thirty minutes prior. He carefully maneuvered the pitchers past the clusters of mountain-men patrons and their company.

Slipping through the crowds, Gale plopped into a red leather booth at the back where Lambert was waiting with Lucy.

As Gale settled into the cheap, frayed leather, he asked Lambert, "Is this really what we had in mind? Cheap vices and awful music?"

"As I recall, this was Bohden's fantasy. I'm just here for the people-watching." As Lambert said this, he poured a small amount of his beer into a bowl for Lucy, who went at the foamy brew like a hyena to carrion.

"That can't be the best for her diet," Gale said.

"She needs it more than us. Poor girl deserves to give her nerves a break after all we've put her through."

Empathic to Lambert's words, Gale reached to give Lucy a rub on the head. She in turn looked up and gave a subtle growl. Both perplexed and frustrated, Gale backed off and wondered aloud, "What is it exactly? You would think after all these years that she wouldn't keep doing that."

"Too much time hiding behind that scope, Gale; you never got to know her like the rest of us."

"It's not my fault. Selection placed me there . . . only thing I was good at. Maybe you could tell her that."

"Why don't we try something less complicated," said Lambert, reaching into his pocket to grab a handful of dog treats to pass to Gale.

As Gale adjusted himself and held out his offering, Lucy looked to Lambert and then placed her paw on his forearm. "Don't try that on me, you sneak. Just go get it."

After Lambert released her, Lucy cautiously inched her way across the table and ate the treats from Gale. With a hesitant hand, Gale softly rubbed Lucy between the ears.

"Feel better?" Lambert asked.

Gale just smiled.

Across the room, Bohden emerged from the crowds, drunkishly shoving himself through them as he headed for the group. As he sunk into the booth, his defeated demeanor gained everyone's curiosity.

"How bad is it?" Lambert asked.

As Bohden slumped farther into the leather, he told the table, "I guess she got the courts to rule in her favor over six months ago. All my accounts are drained, and she remarried some wanker from France. . . ."

"From France?" Lambert said, wincing.

"Aye. Can you believe that?"

"I don't understand. How could she remarry without you signing papers?" Gale asked.

"Find a good enough lawyer and everything is legal, mate."

Upon noticing Bohden's sluggish words, Lambert asked, "How much have you drank already?"

"What's it matter how much I drink? Got nothin' left, anyway."

"That's where you're wrong. You've got your

freedom . . . freedom from two wars by the sound of it."

"Eh, what do you know. You ain't ever been married. You ain't even touched a woman since I've known ya."

"'Course not. Because then I'd end up like you." Lambert's remark gave Bohden exactly what he needed: a good laugh and a smile. But the revelry was cut short by Arlo's arrival.

"Arlo! You made it!" said Lambert, who was then cut down by Arlo's stoic reply, "I need to speak with you all."

Gale replied to his joyless leader, "Take a seat, then. Lambert was just about to enlighten us on the futility of romance."

"Outside," was all Arlo said before turning and leaving the table. Lambert, Bohden, and Gale gave each other shared looks of confusion before following.

Arlo emerged through the rusted alley door that led out of the tavern. The ground was damp and glistening from the late afternoon rain that still clung to the asphalt.

Lambert and Lucy were the first to follow Arlo out. Not far behind was Gale and Bohden, the latter of which stumbled more than he walked. "Wait, I think I get it now," said Bohden. "I can't call the kettle black because I'm also a kettle."

"Technically you're a pot, but you're on the right track," replied Gale as he helped Bohden stand straight for the meeting.

"What's a pot got to do with this?" Bohden asked.

It was at this point that Lambert assumed the worst. "Why do I sense that our celebration over?"

"Why, what's happening?" Bohden asked as he braced himself against the cinder block wall.

With only a few hours before midnight, time was running out, so Arlo laid it out with cold detail. "Caylen gave up the location of the Minuteman; he's held up in a compound near the Neutral Zone, in Colony A-13. A local asset has provided visual confirmation and they are mobilizing to go in and get him. Sheridan has asked us to lead the raid, but if we end our service tonight, then the mission will go to Wallcroft."

Lambert ground his teeth and shook his head in disbelief. "Un-fucking-believable. Let him have it, Arlo. It's not our problem anymore."

"I'm sorry, but I can't just forget what he did

yesterday. I can't let someone like that finish what we started."

Even in his drunken state, Bohden composed himself enough to reason with Arlo.

"The papers are signed and submitted. It's already over. We're free men. They can't order us to do anything."

"You're right. Nobody can order you to take this mission. It's voluntary."

Lambert knew Arlo well enough to sense he was hiding behind double-speak. "Don't try and guilt us into this. You really think the Americans will quit just because they lose one man? Do you honestly think that someone won't take his place?"

"This will end if the Minuteman surrenders, which we can achieve with his capture."

"How many times have we heard that line, Arlo? 'You men have changed the war'; 'the war is almost over'; 'one more sacrifice for King and Country.' What's different this time?"

"What was the point of everything we've fought for, if we just let a psychopath ruin it? Because that's exactly what's about to happen if we don't take this."

Compelled to make his case, Bohden began

blurting out, "I don't know what you fought for, Arlo, but I did what I did because I was ordered to. That's what happens in mandatory service. What you're talking about isn't mandatory."

Still shaken by what Arlo was asking, Lambert attempted an appeal to logic. "Do you not remember how bloody long we trained just to get Caylen? We rehearsed that entire op for a month. Even if we agreed, how the fuck are we supposed to prep for something like this? I mean, are they out of their fuckin' minds?"

"I understand what you're saying, but if we don't move now, then he can vanish again."

A quiet but convicted response then came through the silence that had set in.

"I'll do it." Gale said in a humble voice. "I may be free, but I still have to live in this world. If Wallcroft takes our place for this . . . nothing will be clean; nothing will be right. All that will come from this is probably a martyr who will rally thousands, if not millions. That means more bombings, more killings, and it probably won't stop there. Freedom won't matter at that point. The Crown will lock down every free street and corner, just like they did at the start of all this."

"Fuuuuccc—" slurred Bohden as he was taken by Gale's sentiments. "Why the effin' speech, mate? It's always the speeches. . . ." Bohden's tone made it evident that Gale's words changed his mind.

"Is that a yes?" Arlo probed.

"Aye . . . aye, I'm in. . . ."

Furious yet conflicted, Lambert hurled his glass against the wall in protest as he told the group, "I did my time. If you all want to ruin the lives you've been given back, then go ahead, but I won't have any part of it." Lambert began walking down the alley. Lucy followed with her tail low and her eyes worried. After several steps, she looked back at the other three they were leaving behind.

.   .   .

That night, Arlo slipped into the depths of a lucid dream. The trance-like vision began with him and an unknown team of special forces members, all of which were onboard a helicopter rushing to respond to a crisis that not even Arlo knew of. Every soldier besides Arlo was anonymous in appearance. All were masked in black, and their eyes were hidden by night vision goggles. Obscuring everything further was the dim red light of the cabin that did little to help Arlo discern the strange, hypnotic realm. Adding to the ominous state was an aberrant and indiscernible radio chatter coming from the cockpit. The static voices were like whispers from a ghost. "Where are we going!?" asked Arlo to one of the soldiers beside him, who responded with silence.

As the helicopter throttled down and lowered in altitude, Arlo's instinct provoked him to open the sliding door of the cabin. At first, he gazed out at the city of London lit up against the night, but the spectacle didn't last. In a collapsing pattern, a blackout of the city occurred. One by one, every power grid fell in a chain reaction until no light remained except for the single block of the city Arlo was approaching.

With a sweeping maneuver, the helicopter circled the illuminated area before aligning for landing. This prompted Arlo to lean over and observe the complex. He noticed that the buildings and the layout were familiar to him, prompting him to realize that it was the Imperial Palace. With a sudden rise of anxiety, Arlo stiffened and readied himself. He glanced over the elegant horseshoe pattern of the compound. Much to his concern, the roof and open courtyard were littered with bloodied and mangled corpses.

After finishing the flight path and settling to a hover above the courtyard, the helicopter lowered in a vertical motion and landed upon the marble ground. Once touchdown was complete, Arlo leaped out and readied his rifle.

As if guided by an unseen hand, Arlo led the team to the giant metal doors of the front entrance. Along the way, Arlo scanned the many corpses, noticing that they were torn open from the inside, as if something had emerged from within and left the body like discarded skin.

When Arlo reached the front doors, he ordered the nearest man to pull them open. Cautious and vigilant, he stepped into the main hall of the palace and continued under the giant British flag hung from the ceiling. As Arlo gazed upon the flag, he was both mesmerized and stricken with horror as a fire with no origin burned it up. Not a moment later, his team succumbed to the same fate. Each soldier wailed with agony and cried out as flames consumed their bodies. The dream state paralyzed Arlo, crippling him from action and forcing him to watch.

Just before the fire consumed the last man, his blazing body walked toward Arlo. With nothing but a skeleton remaining, the soldier's charred skull commanded Arlo, "You must save the King."

Following the soldier's words, the floor under Arlo cracked and broke apart from a sudden seismic split, but not before a rope fell quickly from an ethereal sky and allowed him to descend through the shattered ground and into the abyss beneath. As he continued down the rope, shards of broken earth lingering in the air assembled to create the royal throne room.

When Arlo reached the surface, the palace was miraculously constructed from the floating debris with enthralling detail. Royal columns formed beside a red velvet carpet that led to the steps of the throne where the King himself was seated with golden garments.

Upon seeing Arlo's desperate approach, the King stood and gracefully walked toward him. The long fabric of his royal gown dragged behind as he descended the velvet stairs. Just before Arlo could reach him, the King began to collapse amidst the sound of snapping bones and stretching tissue. The frightful sound was as if something was hatching from within. Arlo watched as the King's flesh was then ripped apart to reveal a metallic humanoid beneath. As the machine clawed out of the King's corpse, its hydraulic- and piston-driven frame became visible amidst the layers of blood-drenched flesh. Once the cybernetic figure was standing, it turned its box-like head toward Arlo and haunted him with a gaze from the many lenses it had for eyes.

.   .   .

Arlo jolted awake in bed. His body was drenched in sweat, and a cold chill leaked all the way into his bones. After realizing the surreal vision was nothing but a dream, he was comforted by the familiar sight of the barracks. He then turned to see that Bohden and Gale were asleep across the way. Or so he had thought.

"Bad dream?" asked Gale.

"Yeah, something like that," muttered Arlo in disbelief.

CHAPTER 3

Brilliant rays from a rising sun crested over the mountains surrounding Fort Hutchinson. The early hour was met with heightened activity on the base that came in the form of a colossal transport plane occupying the main runway. Its massive silhouette was carved out by a rim of light that emanated from the sunrise. Juxtaposed were the busy shadows of the maintenance team as they tended to the necessary preparations on the aircraft.

Arlo, Gale, and Bohden had endured the long night of mental rumination that resulted from their decision to accept the mission. Each man managed only an hour of sleep, but that was nothing they were not used to. Especially for Gale who was a veteran insomniac and seasoned night owl.

The team of three were assembled in the all-too-familiar situation room, the same four walls they assumed they would never see again. The entire setting was covered in topographic maps, as well as pictures and descriptions of notorious and wanted American loyalists. Ironically, most of the individuals listed were either put down or put away at some point by Arlo's team.

"What did everyone do with their discharge papers?" Bohden began as he tried to pass the silence of awaiting Sheridan's arrival.

"Never opened mine," said Arlo.

"What about you, Gale?"

"Tossed 'em. We'll get new ones," he said as he paced the room, studying its details.

Realizing where Bohden was leading with his questions, Arlo cut ahead, saying, "I assume you wouldn't have asked, unless you wanted to share what happened to yours. . . ."

"Well, that's the funny part. I can't find mine."

"You lost them?" Gale said.

"It was an unusual night. Don't you remember?"

"Do you?" teased Arlo with a mocking smile.

The humor Bohden fostered was abruptly choked off by the arrival of Sheridan and his dutiful stride into the room. Upon first sight of the Colonel, Arlo, Bohden, and Gale stood up to salute. Following just behind

Sheridan, however, was the unexpected entrance of Wallcroft and his team of five Legion soldiers.

Arlo's heart sank; his surprised state then fast gave way to a contained fury as he locked eyes with the antagonistic Captain. Bohden and Gale were no different in their reactions; both felt the same sudden mental rush of betrayal.

"Apparently, I missed something, Colonel?" asked Arlo, who was fighting to maintain his composure.

"I told you this would be a joint operation between us and intelligence, Lieutenant. You two will be setting aside your differences for the duration of this mission."

"Seems I'm not the only one who feels they've missed something. I wasn't aware of any differences between us, Arlo?" said Wallcroft with a disingenuous look of confusion.

"You think I would have agreed to this if I'd known we're supposed to be partners? You held this from me, Colonel," said Arlo as the cracks began to form in his struggle to maintain an officer's poise.

"What's at stake here is bigger than both of you. The American insurgency is about to be crushed, once and for all. If that's not apparent in its severity, then maybe you should rethink your decision to be here."

With Arlo still unable to shake the fog of the sudden dissonance, Wallcroft stepped forward to attempt a resolution for the tension in the room. He held out his hand and proposed to Arlo, "For King and Country, no?"

In the end, Arlo knew he had no other choice. If he walked from the mission at this stage, then the curse of desertion would follow him and crush any hope for a career as a diplomat.

With a fair hesitation and reluctance, Arlo reached over to shake Wallcroft's hand. Arlo murmured back, "For King and Country."

As Arlo let go of Wallcroft's hand, Sheridan began the briefing. "Alright, everyone take a seat. We have a lot to go over."

With a quick press of a remote control, Sheridan powered on a computer screen at the front of the room and then moved to pass each soldier a file of papers and images.

As everyone began to study the brief, Sheridan explained how the mission was to unfold. "As I trust you have all been made aware, your target for this mission is the Minuteman himself, whom intelligence has located at a compound 130 miles outside of Colony A-13, near the border of the Neutral Zone."

"If I may ask, sir, why so close to the action? A-13 is still a disaster zone, isn't it?" asked Gale as he reviewed the first pages of the brief with astonishing speed.

"Correct, but he needs A-13 to keep peddling his fiction. It's where he claims to his followers that they will find the supposed evidence of the first American Revolution."

"Why's he looking for something that never happened?" Gale replied.

"Because the man is a radical and a traitor; what more do you really need to know?" said Wallcroft, never lifting his eyes from the brief.

"Agreed," replied Sheridan, who changed the digital presentation to display precision satellite surveillance images of a secluded farm property deep within a sprawling forest—an ideal hideout for a pariah such as the Minuteman. "As you can see from our reconnaissance of the target site, we can't risk insertion by helicopter—too much activity in the hills surrounding the compound. American fortifications on the east and west sides will hear you coming and alert the area. With that being said, I've arranged for your teams to infiltrate via high-altitude jump. Both teams will depart from here at 1800. That puts you at the drop zone by 2200, which I've marked on your maps. It's an open field about a mile and a half south of the compound. Once you've completed the jump and you're on the ground, you will proceed on foot to apprehend your HVT."

As the room processed the technical details of what was to come, Sheridan exhibited concern for what he was about to say. "Now, there is a complication. Based on our latest report from the interrogation, the Americans have learned to crack our radio encryption, which means that once you make the jump, a comms blackout will be in effect."

Puzzled by the order, Arlo immediately locked eyes with his team. After they exchanged their looks of concern between one another, Arlo said to Sheridan, "No radios? How are we supposed to call for extraction, sir?"

"Myself and an intelligence team will be observing the mission from an ISR feed. Once you make the grab, bring him to the center of the compound and I'll send in the extraction team. Simple as—" Sheridan's attention was abruptly pulled to the door at the back of the room.

"Sorry I'm late," said Lambert as he casually wandered into the briefing with Lucy beside him. As Lambert took a seat behind his teammates, he saw that each of them was containing a smile beneath their soldier's masks.

As they settled themselves, both Lambert and Arlo could sense that Wallcroft was searching for a vector to exploit the late arrival and, in an effort to detour him, Arlo poised a question to the room: "Do we have anything about where the Minuteman may be located in this compound? That's quite a lot of acreage to cover."

Wallcroft was eager to answer, saying, "Our estimates place him in the southern structure that we believe is a troop-housing quarters. From the ground it will look like a barn."

"Interesting. Are there any other estimates that you could share with the rest of us?" replied Arlo with a cautious concern for what had been withheld up until now.

"If any come to mind, I'll be sure to voice them,"

Wallcroft concluded with a smug grin.

Before the many personalities of the room could clash again, Sheridan steered the briefing back on course. With a commanding voice, he told both teams, "Let's talk rules of engagement. Recon shows that the compound is defended mostly by local militia, which means you can expect light to moderate resistance. The night will be your biggest advantage here. The Americans have always struggled to fight in the dark."

"May I ask for the final verdict on whose jurisdiction this operation falls under?" Wallcroft said, his words deliberate as he searched for any weak point to exploit in Arlo's leadership. It was a clever play in the game of hierarchical dominance that Arlo wanted no part of. However, Arlo responded accordingly, with silence. Refusing to take the bait.

"The SAS will be leading this with cooperation from intelligence, which means Lieutenant Shaw will be the ranking officer in the field, followed by you. Is that understood?"

"Perfectly," replied Wallcroft with a nod.

With the briefing complete, Sheridan stepped forward to offer his final words. "I know the talking heads and the media have spun this war to seem futile. They want us all to believe that we need to move on and forget all those who gave their lives for this. But they don't know our enemy like we do. This ends with the Minuteman, agreed?"

"Yes, sir," they all replied in unison, save for Lambert who mumbled nothing of the sort. Sheridan then concluded, saying, "Dismissed."

After everyone was relieved and left to begin their preparations, Sheridan and Arlo came together in the hallway outside the briefing room. Sheridan spoke to the concerns Arlo was still wearing on his face. "Don't think I don't have my own feelings about this, but you need to understand that my hands can still be tied. This was the best it was ever gonna get."

"My men and I agreed to this because we were replacing Wallcroft, not working with him."

"You want my advice? Try to think of this as a learning experience. If a career in Parliament is still what you want, I can guarantee you will run into plenty more personalities like him. And when it happens, everyone will look to how you handle it. Trust me, I know."

"I just don't understand why it would ever be like

this after what happened?"

"You really want to beat him? End the war. That way, he won't be able to use it as an excuse when the courts deal with him. Understand?"

.　　.　　.

After his brief council with Sheridan, Arlo stepped out onto the base to find all three members of his team waiting for him.

"The hell was that about?" Bohden asked as Arlo joined the group.

Arlo told the others, "He said it wasn't his call, said his hands were tied."

Lambert scoffed and shook his head, "I'm not buying it. He's keeping something from us."

"What do you mean?" Arlo urged.

"Wallcroft thinks he's a better a liar than he is, but he's too desperate for his ambitions, makes him an easy read. He's eager about something. We need to keep as close a watch on him as we can."

Bohden nodded in agreement with Lambert. "You won't hear any argument from me."

Gale being the analytical mind that he was, he connected Lambert's words enough to ask, "Do you think that the Colonel is working with Wallcroft?"

"Don't know for sure; it's possible. Who else could have given the order for Bravo team to stand down from arresting Caylen?"

Arlo quickly interjected, "No, I know the Colonel. If there is anything suspicious, it's coming from above him."

"Hope you're right," Lambert replied with a doubting glance.

. . .

It was late afternoon by the time the team completed their preparations. They spent the hours of the day selecting and fine-tuning their necessary equipment in the open ready room beside the tarmac. Their objective was to remain light and agile, mobile and unencumbered by anything excessive. Each man packed no more than what was needed.

Lambert, the breaching expert of the group, prepped and packed a small demo bag of explosive charges, should they find themselves needing to get through any locked or barricaded doors.

For weapons, Arlo, Lambert, and Bohden selected short-range, close-quarter rifles configured for nighttime operations. Each of their rifles were equipped with suppressors to conceal gunshot volume, infrared lasers for target designation, and optics that would register on night vision.

Gale, the designated team marksman, equipped himself with a longer-range, higher-caliber rifle for engaging at a distance. Additionally, he brought with him a small spotter's scope capable of thermal imaging.

To complete their setup, everyone dressed in combat fatigues, which were a dark and desaturated camouflage. Even the union jack flags the soldiers wore on their sleeves were stripped of color to avoid contrast.

After everyone's bags were packed and zipped, the team found themselves with less than an hour of grace before takeoff. Each man spent the time as they saw fit.

Gale pacified his severe OCD by unpacking his gear, and then repacking it, each time validating that all essential items were accounted for, despite his mind accusing him of forgetting them. Each time he unzipped and unfolded the bags, he would prove to his overly cautious mind that the items were present.

Bohden took a far less neurotic approach by lying down upon the smooth concrete of the aircraft hangar and losing himself in calming tunes of instrumental ukuleles. His less complicated mind found solace in watching the many military aircraft depart and arrive. Accompanying this was Bohden's love for the smell of burning jet fuel that brought him a unique sense of peace.

Arlo and Lambert passed the time by way of their standard tradition, pre-mission debate over a game of darts.

"Would it be too much for me to assume that you came back because you believe in this mission?" said Arlo as he readied for the first toss into the corkboard target.

After Arlo's toss struck near the bullseye, Lambert offered his response. "You want to know what I believe? I think that the three of you needed a sanity check, but by the time I found you, you had already entered the briefing room."

"And this sanity check had to be done in person, with all your gear?"

"It was my intent to be ready for anything."

Arlo lifted his eyebrows as he kindly mocked Lambert's excuse. He then readied another dart for an attempt to break the tie that had formed. "I have a hypothetical for you," he said as he lobbed his second shot. "Say we capture the Minuteman and end the war. And what if, without the Americans dividing us, society comes together, and we usher in a new era of unity and progress. Will you still live in isolation on a cattle ranch?"

"Absolutely."

Lambert's answer prompted Arlo to grin from the familiar feeling of wrestling with Lambert's impossible stubbornness and immovable convictions. "Help me understand, then. Why would you not want to enjoy the success of what we are trying to achieve? The Empire will have no standing enemy. Think of the potential."

"The Americans weren't the first enemy, and they sure as shit won't be the last—which is the real problem. When rulers are threatened, violence is always their answer."

"So, what's your proposal to the problem, then?"

"A new perspective."

"Such as?"

"That there is more to life than putting our hope in government to answer our problems."

"To do anything in life, though, people need security, which Government exists to provide."

"I think you missed my point. Who are we? What are we doing here? Even you have wondered it; I know you have. If you're really looking for a cause to unite us, then that should be it."

"Philosophy has tried that question before, and it has certainly existed alongside government for centuries. Look at the Greeks."

"Believe me, I have. They even had a word for what I'm on about: hypostasis—means the reality behind reality. They knew the world is a chessboard and that everything on it is moved by unseen forces."

"I can't follow you where you're taking this, you know that."

"Then you aren't serious about solving the problem," Lambert concluded, tossing his final dart into the board. "That's game. You owe me a drink . . . again."

As the sharp metal tip punctured the cork board,

the prop engines of the troop transport plane sounded with a loud whistle and began to flood with propulsion. The massive propellers slowly crawled along the bearings until they cycled round and round, eventually spinning up to full idle.

After regathering his team, Arlo led his men out of the ready room and toward the tarmac. The walk from the aircraft was about fifty yards, just long enough for the four men to leave behind any last thoughts of doubt or hesitation for what was to come.

The cargo ramp that led into the back of the aircraft was already lowered and awaiting Arlo's team. As they arrived, they noticed that Wallcroft and his men were already aboard and situated. Once more Arlo gathered himself and composed his professional demeanor to deal with his unwanted nemesis. Arlo gave Wallcroft nothing that his conniving nature could twist or repurpose. No expressions, no emotions, just a neutral and focused face.

Once aboard, a crew chief immediately approached Arlo. He impatiently directed Arlo's team to their places aboard the aircraft, which were harsh canvas seats stretched across metal frames.

As soon as Arlo and his team secured their gear and took their seats, the crew chief moved to do a final check on all passengers. As he passed by, he pulled tight on everyone's restraints and straps.

After everything passed inspection, he moved to the front of the aircraft and gave the pilots up front the all clear.

As everyone awaited takeoff, Lambert mocked the Crown's request for their extended service. "So what do you call your last mission . . . after your last mission?"

"Maybe we should think of a name for it," Arlo added.

"Voluntary punishment," Lambert said as he adjusted the worn nylon straps of his seat. Lambert's words made Arlo smile. It was in this moment that the entire team felt the true gratitude of Lambert changing his mind. For there was no one who could fill his place as the unyielding cynic.

With the preparations complete, the hulking aircraft began to taxi down the access path to the main airstrip where several Imperial fighter jets were landing from a late-hour patrol. The ambient heat from the turbine engines blurred the image of the airstrip into a surreal mirage that floated just above the concrete.

After the runway was clear, the pilots pulled the aircraft into position for takeoff. As the plane came around, the pilots could see the full stretch of flashing runway lights that ran out all the way to the mountain slope.

"Tower, this is Goliath with information foxtrot requesting clearance for takeoff," said the main pilot over the radio.

"Goliath, you are clear for eastbound departure. You have information, foxtrot."

"Goliath copies."

As the pilot finished his call to the radio traffic controller, he slowly brought the throttle controls forward and increased power to the engines. With this, the props spun up to maximum. Once the engines were level and holding, the giant aircraft accelerated down the runway and took flight into a twilight sky.

CHAPTER 4

It was almost two hours since the takeoff from Fort Hutchinson and the late summer sun completed its descent beyond the horizon. The clear and open sky was a dark velvet that was fading into a soft gradient of nightfall.

As the flight entered Colony A-13 airspace, every soldier was silent and in their own thoughts. They contemplated the steps of the mission, envisioning how they would move through each phase, all the way from the jump to the capture, and then finally to extraction.

Gale was the only odd man out of the bunch. For the entire flight, he remained immersed in his favorite pastime, reading the literature of the old world. Aided only by a dim red cabin light, he was within range of the last chapter, but his read was cut short as the crew chief stood and shouted to the teams, "One minute!"

To survive the low oxygen of high altitude, every jumper attached a breathing mask to their helmet fasteners. As Arlo powered on the automatic flow and respirator, he recalled the old days of cumbersome manual tanks and valves. Everything they used now was machine assisted and automated, a trend that he was noticing more and more as the Legion grew in priority and influence within the Crown.

With less than a minute before the drop, the crew chief made his way to the back of the plane to lower the cargo ramp. His hand pressed and held down a large glowing red button. Massive mechanical levers sounded and rumbled as the gigantic back door of the aircraft lowered to reveal the open night sky.

Wallcroft and his men were first to stand for the jump. As they did, they arranged themselves into single file. Directly behind them, Arlo and his team did the same, stacking themselves in a column of Bohden, Gale, and then finally Lambert, who attached Lucy to his body with a custom dog harness. The final step was for Lambert to secure a set of goggles around Lucy's eyes to protect her vision from the forceful winds of the free-fall.

"Thirty seconds!" urged the crew chief to the

jumpers. As the last seconds approached, Arlo gazed past Wallcroft and into the endless horizon, illuminated by nothing more than the ever-fading pink glow of the now-distant sun. When the clock reached zero, the harsh red light above the cargo door shifted to a luminous green. One by one, Wallcroft and his men leapt out in a synchronous rhythm. With the first team out and away, Arlo then led his own men to the threshold.

Arlo, a veteran jumper, turned to give a familiar and confident thumbs up to his team. Each responded with an assuring nod. "For King and Country," said Arlo against the rushing wind, to which his team echoed, "For King and Country."

Arlo initiated a radio transmission and told the other end, "London, this is Paladin, going dark."

Everyone then switched off their radios and stepped toward the edge. With courage rising in his heart, Arlo took the leap off the platform, and into an ethereal sky. Mere moments behind was Bohden, Gale, and then finally Lambert with Lucy.

There was a liberation that came with a free-fall jump. The leap from the platform was always a leap into a new world, a focused world, one with neither the static of normality nor the incessant chatter of its perpetual presence. All of Arlo's anxieties and worldly fears were relegated to a silent stasis. Anything but the jump was drowned out by the necessity of the present.

Each soldier was equipped with an altimeter on their wrist that informed them of their distance to the ground. As Arlo descended, he kept his eyes on the needle, waiting for it to reach the ideal zone of 37,000 feet. Steadily the gauge approached the number and as soon as it was within range, he reached to grab his pilot chute. After the wind took the fabric, the full canopy came next. The sprawling canvas rushed out from the pack and deployed perfectly into the air, sounding with a loud, whipping boom.

Following in a seamless and rhythmic row, Bohden, Gale, and Lambert all did the same. After every canopy was deployed, all that remained was the long, ghostly glide down into the realm of the enemy, some twenty miles away.

.   .   .

From an airborne view, the drop zone was easy for the

team to spot. Arlo could see the familiar landmarks that surrounded the open meadow, the same ones highlighted in the mission brief. There was a jagged mountain range to the north, and a massive lake to the west.

Arlo positioned himself to be the first to land. Upon settling into his final approach, his hands pulled and yawed the cables of his chute to guide himself in. Once his feet made contact with the soft soil, he ran forward through the waist-high grass to resolve the momentum of landing. With well-trained hands, he turned around and pulled in the chute to prevent it from being taken by the wind. Bohden was the next one in. He did the same as Arlo, as did Gale, and then finally Lambert, who had the more difficult task of landing with Lucy who, despite her many jumps, preferred insertion by helicopter over parachute.

Each soldier moved with professional haste as they shoved their canopies back into their packs, careful not to clang the metal buckles that could be easily recognized by any nearby patrols or watchmen. The final step of the landing was to engage their night vision, which they did by lowering a set of goggles from the forward-facing hinge of their helmets. With a quick turn of the power dial, every team member saw a bright green landscape, clear as day. Finally, each of the four unstrapped their rifles and checked the holographic optics to make sure their reticles were visible through night vision.

Despite the smooth landing, Bohden was the first to notice that something was off. "Arlo, where's Wallcroft?"

Prompted by the anxious question, Arlo looked all over. "Shit, does anybody see them?"

Each member of the team began to investigate the area, but there was nothing—only the stillness of the trees, and the constant quiet hum of insect life in every direction.

"I got nothing," said Lambert with a hesitant enthusiasm.

"Did they move out already?" Bohden asked.

By this time, Gale had completed his search of the field and informed everyone, "I don't see their packs anywhere."

After piecing his thoughts together, Arlo queried the others. "You think they missed the drop?"

"Probably missed it on purpose. I told you he was

up to something," said Lambert, true to his conspiratorial thinking.

With no sign of Wallcroft, Arlo grabbed his radio switch, but was abruptly stopped by Bohden reminding him, "Chief, the blackout, remember?"

"Shit. . . ." Arlo muttered as he pulled his hand away from the radio.

"What are we supposed to do?" said Gale, looking to Arlo for leadership, who then turned back to his team saying, "Suggestions?"

Lambert was quick to offer his thoughts. "Best-case scenario, him and his team got lost and won't get in our way. We complete the mission and leave him for search and rescue. Worst case, he's already at the target site and probably already cleaned up."

"Think we can we do this with just four of us, then?" asked Arlo, searching for the assurance he wanted from the others.

"Wouldn't be the first time," Lambert replied.

Arlo debated his options. In many ways, this is what he'd wanted all along, for Wallcroft to be out of the picture. Moreover, Lambert was right, it would hardly be the worst thing to have happened—far from it if he counted every time they had been dealt a rotten hand during an operation. He eventually voiced his decision. "Alright, we proceed as planned. On me."

After giving the order, Arlo stood up and led his team toward the compound. Each man followed close behind until they entered the tree line and faded from view like specters of shadow.

.   .   .

It took roughly thirty minutes for Arlo's team to make it from the drop zone and through the aphotic forest that surrounded the Minuteman's compound. As they came upon the perimeter of the area, the tree line gave way to uneven and unkempt fields of tall grass.

Settling to a knee among the obscuring weeds, Arlo adjusted the focus of his night vision goggles to better glimpse the distant buildings some hundred yards away. Upon his first scan of the area, Arlo grew concerned by the apparent stillness and lack of American soldiers. Lambert, who witnessed the same, cautiously inched his way to join Arlo's side.

"Anything?" Lambert whispered.

Arlo shook his head and replied, "No one."

"Gale said the same. He can't find anyone."

"Something's not right. This place is supposed to be crawling. Where is everyone?"

"Sleeping. . . . But with our luck, that seems doubtful."

"No. Someone would be on watch."

"What if they got tipped off that we were coming? Maybe they bailed before we got here."

"How, though? Sheridan has reconnaissance all over the area. Wouldn't he have spotted that and called it off?"

"Only other option would be Wallcroft, then."

"Agreed. Bring the others over."

At Arlo's command, Lambert turned to wave at nothing but the forest. Gradually, a mix of weeds and grass moved back and forth from a slight disturbance. Eventually, two wraith-like figures, Gale and Bohden, emerged from perfect concealment. In near-total silence, they moved to join Arlo and Lambert. Once settled, Arlo quietly asked of Gale, "What do you think?"

"I swept the whole compound on the thermal. It's all cold."

As Arlo pondered the next move, Bohden added, "First Wallcroft goes missing, and now this?"

"It's also possible that Wallcroft could have nothing to do with this; it could just be a trap set by the Americans," replied Gale.

"With nothing on thermal, though?" Arlo shot back.

"There are ways to trick the imaging," said Gale.

"But only Crown Intelligence has that kinda tech," Lambert said, insinuating Wallcroft's involvement.

"True, but we have underestimated the Americans before. Remember Operation 30?" Gale asked, prompting Arlo to silence the wayward theories in his mind.

"Alright, we need to find out what's going on. Gale, I want you take up a position on overwatch and cover us while we sweep this place."

"Got it," answered Gale, who rose from the grass and began to glide silently toward a position that overlooked the compound.

As Gale moved into position, Arlo detailed his plan to Lambert and Bohden. "We'll start the sweep from the east, but like Gale said, to avoid another Operation 30, let Lucy get a pass on the buildings, see if she picks up any IEDs. Once we clear the outer set, we'll move in and take the main structure."

Bohden and Lambert nodded in approval, having nothing more to add.

"Alright, let's do this," Arlo concluded.

As the team approached the first section of the compound, their chemistry as a cohesive unit was impeccable. No sector or corner was left unwatched. At all times, there was a set of eyes and a gun barrel in every direction.

Crossing the outermost field, the veil of night drained back to reveal the first set of structures. Upon first glance, the team could see that everything was composed of aging wooden walls standing upon old foundations of overgrown foliage. The untamed nature of the area could not help but provoke speculation that it had been abandoned for some time.

As they came closer to the first building, Arlo moved with heightened caution, slowing down the pace of the approach until eventually leading everyone to take a knee. Arlo then gave Lambert a signal to send Lucy in.

"Lucy, trace," whispered Lambert to his attentive companion, who moved with a prowling posture through the grass. She began sniffing and hunting for explosive residue that could be lingering in the area.

As Lucy traced the perimeter of the building, Lambert noticed that there was a window on the wall nearest to him. He signaled Arlo with his hand that he was moving to check it. Arlo nodded in response and Lambert slowly approached with his rifle aimed and ready.

Much to his disappointment, Lambert saw nothing but an empty stillness on the other side. Neither movement nor sound. He shook his head with a discouraged look and pulled back to signal the group that there was nothing to report.

By this time, Lucy had returned to Lambert, who studied her face. "What did you find, girl? Anything?" Lambert knew from her calm posture that the site was clear. He then spun his finger in the air to prompt Arlo and Bohden to continue with the breach.

As they approached, all three soldiers closely hugged the wall, careful not to expose themselves as they came around the corner.

Upon arriving at the frayed frame of the front door, the team came to a stop, awaiting Arlo's order. Still cautious of the silence, Arlo glanced through the compound, but the same eerie stillness was present. Arlo then gave Bohden a nod to proceed with the breach.

Bohden stepped out from his position and quietly reached for the doorknob. He gave it a subtle turn, checking to see if it was locked. To his surprise, the handle turned all the way until the weathered door was free. Bohden then carefully and cautiously pulled the door back just enough to allow Lambert and Lucy to enter.

As Lambert stepped in, Lucy stuck close to him, awaiting any command that he may give. From one side to the other, they checked and cleared every direction like seasoned masters. Their movements were focused and surgical. Following in only seconds behind was the rest of the team, Arlo being the last to enter.

With the aid of night vision, each member was able to maneuver the pitch-black room with relative ease. In front of them was a small living space with a worn-out couch and blankets. At the other end of the room, there was a ragged kitchen and dining area. As Arlo and Lambert inspected the setting, Bohden moved to cover the only hallway there was, should a threat arise from the back halls.

Curious about the disheveled couch near him, Lambert pulled his glove and leaned over to touch the blanket and pillows. "Cold," he grunted with disappointment.

Arlo then scouted the kitchen, only to discover plates and dishes layered with what appeared to be rotten food. Perplexed by the sight, Arlo ran his gloved fingers across one of the bowls. As his hand pressed the surface, he noticed it was covered in spider webs that glistened in his goggles. "The hell is going on?" he asked as he wiped the webbing onto his pants.

"What is it?" Lambert asked.

"It's all rotten," replied Arlo.

"That doesn't make sense," Bohden added.

"Let's check the back," Arlo commanded as he guided the team onward.

To finish clearing the building, they needed to secure the hallway and the connected rooms. Quietly, the group moved back into a tactical column with Lambert at the lead. Within several steps, they came to the first of two doors.

Lambert cautiously grabbed the handle and then

turned the knob all the way, slowly pushing the door open. With his free hand, he held his rifle up and ready. Through his goggles, he saw his rifle's green infrared laser as it moved across the room. At first, it passed along the wall and then across a set of empty, disheveled beds. When the laser reached the other side, there was nothing but stacks of emptied and torn apart military supply crates. "Clear," whispered Lambert, who crossed the doorframe and entered the room.

Immediately, the team checked for signs of warmth on the beds as well as for any hint of recent American presence. Realizing the fabric was again cold to the touch, Lambert shook his head and whispered, "Nothin'."

The team's focus then moved to checking the supply crates for anything that might tell them what had happened. Upon close inspection, Arlo realized the crates were shaped and configured to store weapons and ammo, all of which appeared to have been taken with the Americans long ago, given the abrasive layers of dust and erosion.

Discouraged, but not yet finished, Arlo signaled for the team to finish clearing the building. He stepped out and took the lead, guiding everyone down to the last room of the hallway. He was quicker this time, less patient. As he came to the final door, he opened it and again found nothing but traces of abandonment. Chairs and tables were aged with cobwebs. Boxes, and crates were left open at some distant point in the past.

As Arlo stepped closer to engage with the mystery, Lambert moved about the room, eventually finding that the entire wall beside him was overtaken by vines and moss. He pulled on some of it. "Either they were happy living like this, or they haven't been here for months," Lambert said as he tossed down a handful of overgrowth.

"Visual confirmation on sight. . . . What a bloody cock-up," Bohden said derisively at the sight of what Lambert found.

"Also not the first time intelligence has fucked us," replied Lambert.

"We're not finished. We still need to check the other buildings," Arlo demanded, despite the evidence before him.

"Check for what, Arlo? They're gone," replied Lambert, urging Arlo to come to reason.

"I don't care. We finish the mission," was all Arlo said as he moved to leave the room.

Lambert grabbed Arlo by the vest and pulled him back. "There's nothing out there, Arlo. Accept it."

"I don't know about that," Bohden said quietly. He directed everyone's attention to a strobing infrared laser.

"That's gotta be Gale," said Arlo as he noticed the triplet rhythm of the laser aimed at the barn house in the center of the compound. "Let's move," he said, commanding his team back together.

Revived with the hope that there was still something they could find, Arlo quickened the pace as he rushed from the derelict house and into the grass field, which ran to the center of the compound.

Though his heart was now racing, Arlo kept the pace quiet, moving with just enough speed and skill as to not break the stealth they had been tactically maintaining.

Shortly into the pursuit, Arlo noticed that Gale's strobe ceased, causing him to slow the team and reduce their steps to careful, balanced movements. Once he came to a halt, Arlo noticed the figure of a soldier crossing the side of the barn. The figure stopped. Arlo quickly realized it was Gale, who had repositioned himself and was waiting for the team.

Abruptly, Arlo closed the remaining gap between him and the barn, whispering with urgency to Gale as he arrived, "What are you doing?"

Instead of replying, Gale pointed to the building, suggesting Arlo listen to what was taking place inside. At Gale's direction, Arlo and the rest of the team heard the muffled screams of a man being tortured and interrogated. Following each plea for mercy, they could hear Wallcroft's unmistakable voice screaming at the man for answers.

"Motherfucker," muttered Lambert with teeth-grinding fury in his voice.

"Did you see him?" Arlo pressed.

"Saw him and two others drag someone in there."

"They must assume we're not here yet, then. Everyone stack up. Gale, I want this recorded for the courts; roll your helmet cam."

"On it," Gale replied as he powered on the small video camera attached to his helmet.

Once the camera was rolling, Arlo gave the signal for his team to move into position for a breach. Bohden and Lambert promptly glided toward the main door and took up positions along the front wall of the barn.

"Lucy, ready," whispered Lambert as he held her by the collar, eager to unleash her upon Wallcroft.

Once everyone found their place, Arlo moved to check the handle of the door. He gave it a soft turn and realized it was locked. As Arlo stepped back, the whole team could hear the interrogation escalating. The shouting devolved into inaudible pleas of pain. Wallcroft screamed back, demanding the hostage to "Give it up!"

With the screams now reaching a critical need for intervention, Arlo gave a nod for Bohden to breach. The six-foot-three giant swung out from his position and bashed the door frame open with the force of his colossal boot. Immediately, Arlo rushed forward, weapon at the ready.

As Arlo crossed the door frame and entered the barn, a dissonance overtook him. There was nothing, no interrogation, no hostage, no voices. "What the hell?" asked Arlo as the rest of the team came following in from behind.

"Lucy, search," grunted Lambert at the sight of the empty barn. As Lucy moved to prowl the empty horse stalls, Arlo and his team did their own inspection. Each soldier carefully scanned a sector of the barn, waiting for an ambush from the shadows. But nothing came, just silence and stillness.

A loud metal *ting* sounded in the middle of the room. Something was dropped from the rafters above, a flash-bang grenade. The device hit the floor, detonated, and Arlo's team was struck both blind and deaf by an overpowering flash of white light that came with a crippling ring.

Arlo tried to recover by tearing off his night vision, which made the effects of the flash-bang that much worse. As he stumbled to regain himself, he could just barely see silhouettes rappelling down from the rafters. Once the figures hit the ground, they swarmed upon Arlo and his men like shapeless apparitions in a nightmare. Before Arlo could regain himself, the butt of a rifle was thrust toward his face.

CHAPTER 5

Regaining consciousness, Arlo found himself bound to one of the frayed wooden columns that loosely held up the barn. When his vision returned, he could see that Gale, Bohden, and Lambert suffered the same and were fettered around him.

When Arlo composed himself enough, he softly spoke, "Lambert? You there?"

"Yeah, I'm here," Lambert responded in a dazed tone.

"Where did they go?"

"Fuck if I know. Woke up and they were gone."

A sluggish groan then came from Bohden as he came to, his words slightly slurred as he told the others, "Cheeky fuckers . . . shoulda known."

Gale's voice followed soon after. "Do you hear that? They're outside."

"How many?" Arlo urged.

Gale listened closely, discerning the size of their opposition. "I count at least five."

As Arlo tried to break from the rope bondage, he said to the group, "Wonder why they didn't kill us."

Bohden then gave Arlo a snarky, sluggish laugh. "Don't be so optimistic, chief."

"Anyone see what they did with Lucy?" Lambert asked to anyone who could answer.

"No sign of her," replied Gale with as much sympathy as he could gather.

Determined to think of options, Arlo asked, "Does anyone still have their gear?"

At that moment, a loud thud hit the roof of the barn. The sound was followed by another, and then another. The team looked up to see that there was a glow of fire bleeding in through the cracks of the ceiling wood. "Fuckin' 'ell, they're burning it," said Lambert in panicked realization.

The arid, rotten wood ignited upon impact and spread a scalding shockwave across the roof. It took only moments for the flames to catch and fester and then move down the walls of the barn.

"Anybody got any ideas!?" shouted Arlo as he

again struggled against his ropes.

Lambert was quick to seize on the question. "Just hindsight. I told you we should never have come here."

As the blaze continued to consume the derelict frame of the building, large chunks of smoldering wood came crashing down from the failing structure. Upon impact with the ground, sparks were thrown up into the now smoke-filled air, igniting stacks of hay, as well as the dying pillars that surrounded Arlo and his team.

"Use the wood! Try to burn through the rope!" bellowed Gale as he tried to grab a burning piece of roof with his boot. The tip of his foot could just barely touch the loose boards that fell near him. As Gale reached with his boot, the pieces broke and splintered, spreading the flames out and around him.

With the hellfire burning in every direction, the smoke reached a lethal density and was consuming nearly all available oxygen. Arlo's team coughed and gagged as the scalding toxic air filled their lungs.

"Goddamnit, I'm not gonna die like this!" shouted Lambert with a broken voice as he used everything he had to try to break the ropes.

Just before the certainty of an atrocious demise,

Arlo's eyes became consumed by a surreal phenomenon emerging from the flaming wall of the barn. At first, he tried to shake it from his sight as if it were a delirious apparition summoned from a fleeting consciousness. However, no matter what he tried, the phantasm didn't fade. What Arlo saw was a warping distortion that seemed to bend and twist the firestorm reality. The anomaly moved like a liquid mirror, reflecting, and bending back everything around it. The dancing flames and winding smoke made it even more difficult to resolve what was walking toward him, but Arlo kept his focus upon it. Eventually the spectacle faded back like retreating water to reveal a human figure, a soldier unlike anything Arlo had ever seen. His outfit was modern and well fitted, but his face was covered by a futuristic mask. Small lenses were fixed to the eyes, and a sleek sheet of metal covered the face. A small tube ran under the mask and appeared to be used for breathing.

Once the figure reached Arlo, it spoke to him in a machine-like voice. "Hold still. I'll cut the rope." The figure then pulled a knife and cut Arlo loose. "You can get out over there, just stay low. They are still in the area. I'll get the others," he assured.

At the command of his phantom rescuer, Arlo stumbled forward and toward a small opening in the wall that the fire had burned out. To cross the ardent passage, Arlo shielded himself with his arm held across his face. Once outside, he fell over and began to crawl into the grass, hoping to avoid the sight of the shapeless enemy he assumed was all around.

After making it several yards, Arlo turned to see Lambert and Gale emerge from the blazing barn, which was now completely consumed by fire. A column of near-infinite smoke was rising from the center and blending seamlessly into the black night sky.

Bohden was the last to escape, the anonymous soldier carrying him out of the broken passage. Once Bohden was able to stand on his own, the figure then moved with determined haste to lead the team into the woods. "Follow me and stay low. The fire and smoke should keep us hidden," he said as he moved in a low crouch through the waist-high weeds.

Eventually the sound of the collapsing barn forced everyone to look back. They watched as the fire finally brought the building down into a crashing mess of smoldering debris.

Guiding Arlo's team through the field, the unknown soldier brought them into the nearby forest where they would be hidden from view amidst the density of thick pine. Arlo's team stumbled forward across the tree line and did all they could to hack and cough their poisoned lungs clear. Once the pain reached a level that allowed him to talk, Arlo confronted the mysterious soldier with a gasping, labored voice. "Who . . . are . . . you?"

"You can call me Gideon."

"Not your name. . . . Are you . . . American?" continued Arlo between gasps.

"What does it matter whose side I'm on? Your own countrymen just tried to kill you."

"And how do you know that?" said Lambert whose voice was equally as broken and fragmented from desperate breathing.

"Would you have preferred I leave you there to burn?"

"It certainly would have made more sense. We are at war, after all," Arlo reasoned as he hurled out a heaving deep cough.

Gideon shook his head as he searched for the

words. "Do you really need this spelled out for you? Four of the Crown's finest, mercilessly burned alive at the hands of the ruthless Americans. Parliament to discuss deploying additional troops to the western colonies. That's the headline they will run tomorrow."

"You don't know what you're talking about," said Arlo as an aggression began to take hold of him.

"Then what's your explanation for why they lured you into the middle of nowhere?"

"You're insane. This is all insane. Who are you!?" Arlo responded, lashing out.

Before Gideon could answer, Lambert addressed Arlo. "No. You want to know what's insane? Sending someone back into the field who is supposedly under investigation for war crimes. Or maybe it was ordering a communications blackout during the so-called most important mission of this war."

"Don't feed this conspiracy, Lambert."

"I'm not feeding anything. I told you Sheridan and Wallcroft had an agenda. They played us like a fuckin' fiddle, and this proves it," Lambert replied.

Stricken with disbelief at Lambert's words, Arlo questioned him. "You believe a man hiding behind a mask over your allegiance to your country?"

"I don't give a fuck what he's wearing. What he's saying sounds a lot more like the truth than anything else I've heard about this mission. And by the way, my allegiance is to you! To this team! Not some nation I was forced to serve."

"He wants to flip us. Can you really not see that?" Arlo said.

Frustrated, but not beyond empathy, Gideon told Arlo, "You've been lied to, incessantly. You have a right to be angry, but not with me. What you do from here is your choice. Crawl back to the Empire for all I care. However, if you want to make yourself useful, then maybe consider helping me stop a psychopath before he does any more damage."

"What do you mean?" asked Arlo.

"Tomorrow your country won't care what it takes to win this war. Even if it means setting someone like Wallcroft loose. If we move now, we might be able to stop him."

Arlo and his team lingered in hesitation. Eventually, Lambert said, "Fuck it. I'm in." He stepped forward to join Gideon.

"Lambert, stand down. That's an order."

"Under whose authority, Arlo?" insisted Lambert.

"Don't do this," Arlo cautioned Lambert with a weakened voice, realizing he could no longer hold his team together with Imperial protocol.

"Anyone else?" Gideon asked, prompting Bohden to step past his guilt and take the offer from Gideon. Following just after was Gale who said to Arlo as he passed, "Even if we assume that Wallcroft is alone in this, why hasn't Sheridan sent a response team in? You heard him tell us he would be watching this whole thing on the ISR and yet he has done nothing. Not even a helicopter to scout it."

Still unconvinced, Arlo remained reluctant to join the others. What he saw was far from a rescuer, but was instead a staged plot by the Americans to deceive Arlo's team into defection. And that's when it hit him: If he could expose Gideon as an American agent, he could win back the loyalty of his team and potentially even discover the truth about what had taken place. Confident with playing the role of a double agent, Arlo stepped forward to feign his allegiance.

.   .   .

The night had passed, and the soft glow of a rising sun contrasted the sky enough for the team to follow a massive column of smoke rising from the forest like an omen. Everyone knew the thick black plume was another wake of tragic destruction left behind by Wallcroft, and as such, it was the best place to begin the search for him.

The dim light of dawn evolved into a bright sunrise by the time they came to the source of the smoke; a convoy of five vehicles had been attacked and set ablaze. The smoldering inferno of scorched metal was about a hundred yards from the team's position and easily visible from behind the concealment of the thick forest where they settled to assess the situation.

"Anything moving in there?" asked Lambert as he studied the remnants of what was obviously an American military group.

Gale gave the area several passes with his spotter's scope that had survived the loss of his gear. "No, but this looks pretty fresh. Maybe an hour by my guess."

"I need to check for survivors. Wait here," Gideon

said, slowly stepping out from the trees. As he moved ahead, Lambert gave him a request. "Might help us be more effective if you found some weapons up there."

"I'll see what I can find."

Stepping out from the trees, the familiar ripples of distorted reality began to wrap and cover Gideon. Within several steps, he vanished from view, merging into the forest. Upon witnessing the surreal phantasm, Lambert turned to Arlo and wondered aloud, "Is that what you were talking about?"

"Yeah. He used it to sneak into the barn last night," replied Arlo.

"Not even Crown Intelligence has anything that advanced," said Gale.

"And neither do the Americans," Lambert replied.

"Then where did it come from?" Gale wondered.

After some time of stalking the blazing wreckage, Gideon was confident that Wallcroft and his men had moved on. He disengaged his camouflage and made himself visible, allowing him to wave for Arlo's team to approach.

Gideon then paced about the area, examining the numerous Americans that were gunned down in an apparent attempt to flee the ambushed convoy. Each corpse was face down in the damp mud with bullet holes in their backs.

Bohden was the first to arrive from across the way and, as his eyes fell upon the carnage, he turned to the others. "This certainly looks familiar."

"Agreed," said Lambert as he crouched to pick up a rifle.

"Looks like the local militia," Arlo observed, studying the ragged, improvised appearance of the bodies' clothing.

Gideon gave Arlo a somber reply. "Most of these men were fathers and sons."

"I always hated that the Americans allowed that. Boys have no place in war."

"Is there such a thing as a proper age to fight for freedom?"

"I think there's a proper age to make decisions about your life, especially when it involves war."

"That's because you think like an Imperial. Out here, fathers, not governments, raise their sons. Trust me, they knew what they were doing."

"You seem quite fond of the Americans to not be

a part of them," said Arlo.

"I know you don't believe me, but I'm not interested in taking sides. I'm just here to ensure that things don't get any worse than they already are."

After Gideon said this, he stepped away, refusing to continue the discussion.

At the back of the wreckage, where the heat was tolerable, Bohden was able to pull one of the American corpses out of a vehicle. He turned the fallen soldier over to see that there was nothing left but charred flesh. Not even the face remained. "Looks like some of these guys didn't even try to run. They must have been trapped by the fire," he said.

After glancing over the wreckage one last time, Lambert asked Gideon, "Was this it or were there more of them?"

"It's likely there's a camp nearby. That's probably where they were retreating from, based on the direction of the vehicles."

"Tracks are still fresh. We could follow them back," added Gale as he walked the dirt road that led back into the forest.

Arlo shook his head, telling Gale, "That could be

miles away."

"Not likely. They wouldn't have let them get far," Gideon replied as he moved to follow the jagged mud tracks of the convoy. After several steps, he turned to see if Arlo and his team would follow. "Are you coming?" he asked.

Lambert was once again the first to step forward, followed by Gale and then Bohden, who both recovered rifles from the wreckage.

As Arlo watched his team depart from him all over again, he suppressed his useless anger. There was no point in clinging to his now-empty authority. He knew that if he wanted to reclaim his leadership, he would have to do it by another means.

To make himself useful for what was to come, Arlo recovered a weapon and stepped forward to join his drifting team.

. . .

After cautiously following the tracks for several hundred yards, the loose foliage thickened to become dense weeds and bush life. It was an ideal change of terrain, one that offered a way to cover the approach of the team as they came upon the remnants of the American camp.

Before they were able to glimpse the site, the sound of approaching Imperial radio traffic began echoing around the forest. As the crackling static and inaudible voices came closer, Gideon waved his hand to prompt everyone to find cover. Adjusting to the source of the sound, each soldier moved with a prudent glide to conceal themselves amidst the loose vegetation.

Arlo was the first to spot the source of the radio traffic: two soldiers of the Imperial Legion on patrol in the area. He tried to listen to what they were discussing over the radio, but the distance made it indiscernible.

Just as the Imperial soldiers patrolled past the team, Arlo raised his rifle and used the crude magnification of the rugged optic. Through the scope, he was able to better see the camp, or at least the remains of it.

The few tents left standing were either littered with bullet holes or torn down in the frantic attempt to escape. He then saw that two more troopers entered the camp carrying the bloodied corpse of an American casualty. Arlo followed the soldiers as they remorselessly dragged the body through the bush and eventually heaved the corpse like discarded garbage onto a large pile of other American bodies.

At first sight of the carnage, Arlo had to look away. He then turned to his team members, who were horrified all the same. A disgusted frown formed on Bohden's face as he connected with Arlo's eyes. Arlo then raised his finger to his lips, stressing the need for them to remain silent, should Bohden's quick temper trigger him to act on his own accord.

Arlo went to look once more. This time he saw an Imperial Officer emerging from one of the tents. His stomach dropped as he realized it was Wallcroft, and with him was Lucy, who he dragged with a rope leash and kicked to force a follow. To prevent her from fighting back, her mouth was bound shut with a leather belt.

As Arlo lowered the scope, he was forced to confront a rising sense of doubt. *What if Gideon wasn't lying?* he thought. *What if Wallcroft and Sheridan really were working together to manipulate the war?*

A new possibility then came to Arlo: If he could arrest Wallcroft, there was the slim hope that he could take him in personally, and with the combined evidence of everything that was already collected, there would be enough to claim charges of war crimes with the justice center. The only challenge would be convincing his team to support it.

Eventually, Gideon signaled for the team to come together. Each man slowly backed away to an area where they could regroup and assemble. "I trust everyone got a look at the situation?" said Gideon as everyone gathered around.

"I did, but five Legion soldiers are no small order," Bohden cautioned.

"They haven't acquired us yet; we still have the advantage," Gideon replied.

Concerned about the direction the plan was heading, especially if Wallcroft was killed in the crossfire, Arlo tried to bring another perspective. "We're talking about firing on our own countrymen. Is there not another way?"

"These are the same countrymen who set fire to the barn they locked you in," Gideon interjected with frustration.

To which Arlo asked, "What about your camouflage? Can't we use that to ambush them and force a surrender?"

"I've already reached the limit for the radiation it emits. And even if I could, what are we supposed to do, escort six prisoners through the woods? We'll all be captured by nightfall. We won't have this opportunity again. Not like this," Gideon said, his words finally getting Arlo to nod his head in agreement.

Gale then finalized the strategy. "The only way to do this is for each man to pick a target and engage at the same time. Ambush them."

"Agreed," Gideon replied.

"If it's possible, I would like to get Lucy out of there before that. She'll come if I call her."

"That could risk the ambush," said Gideon.

"If it's worth it to save us, it's worth it to save her. Most of us are alive because of her."

"Alright. Let's do it, then. Each man mark a target, call Lucy, and then we attack in sync," said Arlo before Gideon could argue the proposal any further.

Consensus reached; each team member took up a position near the camp. All five soldiers picked their targets. They accomplished this by signaling to each other with focused hand movements. Once each member was set and ready, Lambert began the fight by letting out a loud whistle for Lucy. As soon as the piercing tone fell upon her ears, Lucy yanked herself away from a startled Wallcroft and dashed with an uplifted spirit toward the source of the whistle.

Within seconds of hearing Lambert's call to Lucy, the Imperials composed themselves and reacted, dismantling Gale's plan of a synchronous ambush. "Contact!" screamed Wallcroft's squadron as they scrambled for what little cover was available within the camp.

As the Imperials dashed across the camp, Gideon remained focused and tracked his target. Just before the soldier in his sights made it behind some supply crates, Gideon opened fire with several precise gunshots that hit his target's head, causing a pressurized eruption of blood-red mist.

With a full gun fight now unfolding, sporadic, desperate shots were fired from the Imperial side in attempts to suppress and interrupt the assault from Arlo's team. Several bullets whizzed and cracked near Arlo's men, but none of them was accurate.

Even amidst the gunfire, Lucy was able to find

Lambert and take shelter near him. As soon as he was able, Lambert tore off her mouth restraints and rope-tied leash. Their reunion was cut short by the cracks and zings of incoming gunfire as the Imperials better dialed in on the location of the team.

Bohden followed up by returning fire, but by the time he did, his targets had retreated behind the cover of a nearby vehicle. The shots from Bohden's rifle zipped past and ripped through several tents and trees. Splintered bark and torn fabric erupted behind the Imperials' position.

Before the fire fight could reach a stalemate, Gale crept behind several rows of trees to reposition for a better line of sight, one that was parallel to the enemy's side. To help distract the Imperials from catching Gale, Arlo unloaded a whole magazine of blind gunfire toward the camp.

Ensuring that the diversion was not interrupted, Arlo shouted, "Loading!" as soon as his rifle was out of ammo.

An answer then came from Gideon, who was the first to respond. "Covering!" he yelled as he leaned out and fired several bursts.

Reloading, Arlo joined back in and continued to engage. Both men fired every shot they could with the hope of trapping the Imperials behind confusion and cover, preventing them from acquiring Gale's movements around them.

Once Gale was hidden behind a growth of tall weeds, Arlo ran out from his hiding place and exposed himself long enough to be acquired.

One of the Imperials fired in Arlo's direction, but not before Arlo vanished from view behind another set of trees. With Wallcroft's men still taking the bait, Gale adjusted his scope for the new distance of his targets. As he aimed, his crosshairs drifted left, up, and then down to find his first target. Once there was a shot acquired, he fired, and the Imperial soldier was killed instantly.

"Contact left! Contact left!" bellowed the soldiers to one another as they tried to locate the direction of Gale's gunfire.

From concealment, Gale fired one precision-timed shot and then another, the deeper tone of the higher caliber impacting soft targets provoked Arlo to lean out from cover and realize that Gale killed off two more panicked Imperials.

Now's our chance, Arlo thought before leaping out from cover and firing several shots at what little remained of the Imperials.

One soldier was killed, but by then, Arlo's rifle was empty again. Just before the Imperials returned fire, Arlo dashed behind cover to reload.

Gale fired another deep, echoing shot. Then Arlo peeked to see that only one Imperial remained. The other was crawling away, only to be fired upon by a follow-up shot from Gale that ripped into the soldier's back, killing him.

The situation was now desperate for the last remaining member of Wallcroft's squadron. His head swiveled and panned in every direction as he frantically tried to locate any sign of Gale in the weeds. In a final attempt to escape, the Imperial leaped from cover to try to make it to the next set of trees, but before he could run three steps, Gideon emerged from behind the tents and fired three precise shots that dropped the soldier to the ground.

Killing their final opponent, Gideon collapsed to a knee, as if he were fighting a sudden loss of consciousness. As he wavered and struggled to stand,

Arlo arrived to lift him by the arm. "You alright?" Arlo asked.

"I'll be fine," Gideon grunted, with a guarded stoicism.

Arlo then stepped away and rapidly checked the bodies in search of Wallcroft. "Fuck! He's not here!" he said as he turned to search the tree line.

Mere moments later, Lambert and Lucy converged at the camp site. As they did, Arlo gave an order, pointing Lambert to Gideon and saying, "Stay with him. I'm going after Wallcroft." Before anyone could argue with him, Arlo dashed into the tree line. Still too weak to chase after him, Gideon let him go.

.   .   .

Some distance from the others, Arlo was moving at a dead sprint through the dense, claustrophobic woods. It was an evolving obstacle course of narrowing passages and fallen branches that Arlo leaped, dodged, and vaulted with an unyielding pace. Propelling him across every pitfall was the fixation that he could not afford to lose Wallcroft.

Arlo made it fifty yards, and then a hundred, but still no sign of Wallcroft. *How could he even have gotten this far?* he thought. With no trail to follow amidst the many diverging directions of the forest, the urgency of the pursuit forced him to gamble on a direction. Just as he stepped forward, the snap of a tree branch followed by a tumbling *thud* sounded from the other direction.

Arlo dashed to where he heard the noise and, as he came bursting through the dangling branches, he saw Wallcroft collapsed on the ground, crippled by a broken ankle. Both men's eyes locked onto each other's and then onto Wallcroft's pistol that had dropped in the fall. Arlo raised his rifle. "Don't fuckin' move!" he ordered, approaching the pistol, kicking it away from Wallcroft's reach.

As Wallcroft tried to rise, Arlo again shouted, "I said, don't move!" But Wallcroft knew he was too valuable to be executed, so he ignored Arlo's demand. As he began to gain his feet, he quickly realized his ankle was shattered and unable to withstand any pressure.

"Well, isn't this just wonderful," muttered Wallcroft with heavy sarcasm in his voice as he realized he could go nowhere.

Arlo marched forward and forcefully yanked Wallcroft, shoving him into a tree trunk. As he ground his face into the bark, Arlo bound Wallcroft into a set of zip-tie handcuffs.

"What exactly are you doing?" asked Wallcroft with a pandering tone, as if he was speaking to a clueless child.

"What does it look like?"

"Like I didn't tie your ropes well enough."

Infuriated, Arlo spun Wallcroft around and slugged him in the mouth, sending a couple of his teeth toward the forest floor behind streams of blood.

"Anything else?" said Arlo as Wallcroft grunted and winced from pain.

"You will hang for treason; I swear it," said Wallcroft.

"Not before you hang for war crimes."

Wallcroft then began laughing and mocking Arlo, telling him, "Is that your plan? You think your word will really mean anything against mine?"

Both Wallcroft and Arlo were then startled by the sound of snapping branches. Gideon emerged from the wall of trees and stepped forward, followed closely by

Lambert, Lucy, Gale, and Bohden.

"He's right. You're wasting time. There's only one way to solve this," Gideon said, pulling his pistol out for an execution.

"No! We need him!" urged Arlo as he leaped to hold Gideon back.

"Need him!? For what?"

"He's going to London to stand trial for his crimes."

"Have you learned nothing from all this? The only thing he'll get there is a medal!"

Wallcroft let out a loud laugh and told Arlo, "He seems to get it, so why don't you? Let the bastard get his fill. It won't undo all I've accomplished."

Taunted beyond his patience, Gideon once again tried to aim his pistol for the kill, but Arlo grappled the weapon from his hand. As he struggled to keep Gideon held back, he spoke to him under his breath, "You're not thinking about this right. If we can expose this in the courts, then it will be public for everyone to see. What better chance for peace between the Americans and the Crown? This is an opportunity for diplomacy, not more bloodshed."

"Are you really this naïve? Do you honestly think the problem is that simple?"

"What's your proposal, then? Kill him and run? Hope that the entire Empire doesn't chase after us?"

"I should have let you burn. . . ."

Before the argument could escalate any further, three Imperial helicopters flew directly overhead. After the thundering black silhouettes passed above the forest canopy, Sheridan's voice came through Wallcroft's radio. "Where are you and your team? You missed the extraction."

A silence fell upon everyone after Sheridan spoke. Arlo thought for a moment; then he reacted by reaching for Wallcroft's radio. As he grabbed it, he opened the channel for a message. "If you want him, then give me the coordinates."

"What are you doing!?" said Gideon after Arlo let go of the switch to close the channel.

"Negotiating," Arlo replied.

"What will it take for you to see the Crown for what it is? You even heard him confess that they tried to kill you."

"I know Sheridan. This is our way out. Just trust

me."

Sheridan's flat, unaffected voice came back over Wallcroft's radio. "There's a field to the southeast of your position. Bring your team and meet me there."

Once the call finished, Bohden offered his concerns, "I don't know about this. . . ."

"No. This will work. I'll meet him alone but you all stay back. Gale can record Sheridan confessing to everything. We can use that to negotiate our safety with the threat of releasing the footage to the Americans."

"What do we do if they start shooting?" asked Gale with genuine concern.

"Shoot back," replied Gideon.

.   .   .

Arlo had done as Sheridan asked and positioned himself in a nearby open meadow of tall grass. He kept Wallcroft close, using him to shield himself should Sheridan try anything but conversation.

Once they were settled in the field, a single Imperial black helicopter made a low sweeping arrival above the trees. The force of the rotors almost flattened the forest canopy as the aircraft banked down for a landing. It touched down and the roaring winds of the rotors settled to an idle.

Sheridan emerged from the main cabin. Escorting him were two of his own personal bodyguards, Imperial Legion by appearance.

Crossing the field, Sheridan kept a cautious distance from Arlo, but was well within speaking range. "Do you know what the punishment is for treason, Lieutenant?" said Sheridan.

"I should ask you the same question."

"Where's the rest of you?"

"My orders were to bring in a criminal. Here he is," replied Arlo as he pressed his pistol against Wallcroft's back.

"Careful. You're about to risk the only chance you have left at a free life."

"I just want to know why. Why this? We're supposed to be above this. It goes against everything we've sworn our oaths to uphold."

"We may be the most powerful empire on earth, but you can only remain that way by acting like it. Sometimes that means getting dirty."

"Dirty enough to stage this whole thing and pin it on the Americans?"

"I did what was necessary."

"Then where does this end? With you? With the Ministry? With the King?"

"What does it matter, Lieutenant?"

"Answer me!"

"We live in the 21st century. Do you really believe that this Empire is run by an old man on a throne?"

"Who, then? Who decided that this was right!?"

"I'll offer you and your team one last chance. Let the Captain go, and we can all go home. I'll wash the records and none of this will matter. That's the best it's gonna get."

"I've heard that enough from you," said Arlo, who then fired three shots into Wallcroft, killing him instantly.

"Goddamnit!" screamed Sheridan as he watched Wallcroft's body fall into the grass. "Kill him!"

Sheridan's men abruptly opened fire upon Arlo, who was dashing across the meadow and toward the tree line. All behind Arlo, the grass and weeds erupted into thick chunks of dirt until the assault was broken apart by

Arlo's men engaging from beyond the trees.

As soon as the Imperials came under fire, they grabbed Sheridan and shielded him with their bodies. With adept skill, they fell back to the chopper, firing a volley of shots into the trees as they did. The countermove was enough to disrupt Arlo's team and buy themselves time to load Sheridan back into the chopper.

Once Arlo crossed the meadow line and was within the coverage of the trees, Bohden noticed that Sheridan was directing one of his soldiers to operate the window-mounted machine gun. Bohden shouted, "Gunner! Gunner!"

In response, both he and Lambert broke away from their positions and began sprinting toward Arlo.

"Lucy, go! Run, girl! Run!" yelled Lambert as he commanded Lucy to sprint ahead and find safety.

After dashing some several yards, Lambert saw that Gale and Gideon were still engaging with the hope of puncturing the rotor head or the engine of the aircraft.

"Gale! Gunner! Move!" commanded Lambert, whose shouting was enough to provoke the men to break away and follow in the fallback.

As the team continued their retreat through the

woods, they felt the full escalation of Imperial force. The helicopter gunner opened fire into the tree line with his six-barreled Gatling gun that roared like a dragon, spewing an onslaught of high-caliber ammunition. It was continuous and unrelenting. Arlo's team sprinted away with everything they had as a path of a thousand bullets pursued the men like a chasing serpent.

Behind them, the entire forest was torn apart by the gunner's fire. Trees were cut in half and the ground itself was almost entirely resurfaced with a storm of sparking dirt and rock debris. Even as the helicopter took flight, the gunner continued the barrage with no sign of letting up. Once the aircraft reached the top of the trees, it banked and turned in such a way as to keep the gunner's assault facing the direction of Arlo's retreat.

After the helicopter settled above the forest canopy, another arrived and maneuvered down to the field for a rapid insertion of more Imperial soldiers. As soon as the landing gear hit the meadow floor, a team of five Imperial reinforcements deployed in a hurry. With the forceful rotor winds at their backs, the fresh team of soldiers rushed to the forest line to pursue Arlo. As they approached the first row of trees, the Gunner's assault stopped, and Sheridan's aircraft retreated from the area.

.   .   .

Weary and weak from post-adrenaline exhaustion, Arlo stumbled and braced against a tree. His breaths were deep and exhausted. He tried to step forward, but his legs were unstable and wobbled.

After resting on the forest floor, Lucy came rushing in to greet him and inspect him for wounds. "I'm alright, girl, I'm alright."

"Arlo!?" bellowed Lambert, in search of him.

"Over here!" he replied as best as his tired lungs could manage. Within seconds, Lambert, Bohden, and Gideon arrived. Their breathing was just as labored and heavy.

"Where's Gale?" Arlo asked in between gasps. His question was answered by the sound of approaching footsteps moving at a dead sprint.

"We got incoming!" Gale shouted as he came rushing in from behind the trees.

"More of 'em?" Arlo asked with urgency as he stood up.

"I counted five, Legion by the looks of 'em," Gale said as he knelt down to catch his breath.

"Quick reaction force, probably one of many on the way," added Gideon.

"We don't have enough ammo for another firefight," Lambert added.

A sudden idea then came to Arlo. "Lambert, you still have those demo charges?"

"Yeah."

"Give 'em here."

Lambert dropped his backpack and unzipped the main compartment. From it he pulled out the first C4 charge he could find. Giving it to Arlo, Arlo tossed it to Gale, saying, "Everyone take a charge, rig it to the trees in a circle around this area. We can funnel them in and blow 'em once they get in range."

Lambert was first to adhere his explosive to the nearest tree. He primed the charge with a small receiver that he pressed into the soft clay-like explosive. Once the charges were set, Arlo's team ran and took cover behind the next row of trees. They had done so with just enough time before the reaction force fell into visual range.

As the Imperial soldiers rushed in, Arlo kept a

focused eye on their movements, waiting for them to come within the necessary distance. Though they were closing in fast, Lambert waited with his thumb just above the detonator switch, holding for the command from Arlo. Just before the first soldier crossed the threshold, he noticed they were starting to drift too far apart and were wandering around the impending blast zone.

"Lucy, speak," Lambert commanded as part of an improvised strategy. Lucy then let out a series of barks that instantly captured the attention of the soldiers, who came charging to the sound, and back toward the trap.

Even after the first Imperial fell into range of the detonation, Arlo waited several more seconds until the rest followed. Once the last soldier cleared the threshold, Arlo shouted to Lambert, "Now!"

Each explosive detonated in a sequential row creating bursting kinetic bubbles of tree bark and ground debris. Once the blast wave flew past Arlo and his men, they peeled from cover and opened fire.

Two of the five soldiers were killed by the detonation; the other three survived but were stumbling to the safety of nearby trees. Their disorientation was evident by their unstable movements as they sluggishly ran from Arlo's team.

Between the steady bursts of gunshots, Arlo shouted, "Displace," prompting Lambert and Gale to run for a flanking position parallel to the enemy. As Lambert fired off a volley of shots, all three Imperial soldiers were forced to fall back and expose themselves. Once they were in the open, Gale fired two precise shots that connected and killed his target.

With the Imperials still on the run, Arlo and Gideon seized the opportunity to emerge from cover and press forward. As they moved, Gideon stopped to toss a grenade. Pulling the pin and throwing it, the small explosive landed with a small *thud* near one of the two remaining soldiers, forcing him to run out and expose himself to another kill shot from Gale.

With only one enemy remaining, Lambert told Lucy, "Take down. Go!"

Lucy charged out in furious pursuit of the final Imperial soldier. Closing the gap, she pounced on her target and closed her heavy bite around his neck. To finish, Lucy yanked the Imperial to the ground. As the soldier fought and screamed, Lambert ordered, "Lucy! Release!" Just as she did, Arlo arrived to finish off the

Imperial with several shots into the center chest.

Arlo lowered his rifle, and the smoke from the barrel dissipated.

Gideon approached him and said, "Seems I was wrong about you."

"I'm not proud of this," Arlo replied.

"No, but at least you're no longer blind to it."

"That's another Imperial chopper headed this way. Do we have any more options left?" Lambert said as he approached Arlo and Gideon.

"The Neutral Zone. The Empire still acknowledges it as a humanitarian corridor. Not even Sheridan will risk violating it with a military incursion. It's about a day's hike, but you can make it with this," answered Gideon as he tossed Arlo a small device that he tore from his vest.

As Arlo looked at the sleek mechanism in his hand, Gideon told him, "It's an infrared scrambler. It will keep Sheridan's drones from acquiring you."

"You're not coming?" Arlo asked.

Gideon shook his head. "Even with that, they won't let up unless we do something. I can lead the rest of the reaction force away with a distraction. Give you all a chance to get out."

"The Legion's a lot to take on. Especially with whatever you're suffering from," said Lambert.

"I can handle myself, but take this also," said Gideon as he released the strap of his watch, one with a large rectangular screen. He swiped the display with this thumb and tapped away at the surface, saying, "I'll input the coordinates for us to meet at The Neutral Zone. Stay on the path; don't wander off it."

Gideon handed the watch to Arlo, who took it and asked, "If we take this, how will you find us?"

"The same way I did last night," replied Gideon, who engaged his camouflage and vanished into the forest. Once invisible, his voice sounded again, telling Arlo and Lambert, "Good luck."

CHAPTER 6

Information moved fast within the Empire. Even faster was the news of failure and defeat among its ranks.

In the wake of Arlo's escape, Sheridan summoned not just his own resources, but the higher echelons of the Crown were reacting to Sheridan's failure, as well. It was only a handful of hours before the wilderness of Colony A-13 was overrun by a storm of Imperial forces.

Near an open meadow where Arlo's team escaped, Sheridan established a mobile outpost hosting the arrival of several squadrons and divisions of the Legion. Alongside the many troop transport helicopters and their respective cargo, intelligence and surveillance equipment were also delivered to the site.

When the assembly was complete, an array of mobile radar and satellite dishes were established and transmitting information to an operations vehicle in the center of the field. It was here that Sheridan tasked a small intelligence team to monitor aerial drone footage of the forest, hoping to find some trace of Arlo and his defiant band.

As Sheridan paced the technology-laden claustrophobic corridor of the mobile war room, his ruminations of Arlo's whereabouts were interrupted by the stentorian sound of an approaching aircraft, one which was noticeably different from anything else that had been through the area. Seconds after hearing the sound, Sheridan made a nervous exit out of the trailer as there was a suspicion he had to confirm.

The aircraft itself was neither helicopter nor plane, but something in between, and hailed from the higher stratum of the Empire. At the end of its elegantly shaped wingspan, colossal turbine engines turned upright to allow for the ship to make a jet-thrusted vertical landing. Once the vessel touched down and the winds settled, a large cargo ramp door at the back lowered to reveal an officer known as Commander Harper. Her attire was regal, as if she had just walked from the courtyards of the Imperial Palace.

As soon as she set foot on the grassy meadow, every soldier and all personnel present abandoned their tasks for a statue-like posture that they dared not waiver from.

She headed for Sheridan with an ominous degree of disciplinary intent on her face. Forced into the presence of a superior officer, Sheridan submitted, and gave a salute.

"I trust you have some kind of explanation for your failure?" scolded Harper in an unusual machine-like voice. As she awaited Sheridan's response, her mechanical eyes stared down the strong-willed colonel.

"Somehow, they've managed to block their signal from our infrared systems. I've sent several teams in on foot to find them. Shouldn't be long now," Sheridan replied with as much neutrality as he could muster.

"Advise your men that when they find them, the traitors are to be captured alive and brought to London where they will be made an example of."

"If they want them alive, that changes things."

"Not for me, nor for my assets."

"Don't threaten me. Both you and your *handlers* know damn well what I've done for this war."

"On the contrary. I believe they would agree with me on the matter, and this disaster you've created is just another reason to justify your replacement."

"Well, thankfully somebody up there still holds your leash."

"For now, but if you fail again . . . the matter will be left to me," Harper cautioned with a blank face.

"I'll get them, the traitors," concluded Sheridan with germane conviction.

.　　.　　.

After separating from Gideon, Arlo's team was guided by his navigation through an arduous day-long hike that was nearing its end. The sun was low and hovering within the trees. Long shadows stretched out across the forest, shaping everything with a harsh contrast, edged by a golden haze.

For all of them, it was the second day of having endured the absence of sleep. The burdensome fatigue that came from no rest was growing heavier with each step they took into what was sure to be another sleepless night.

But despite the gravity of adrenaline-scorched muscles and a near-delirious state of mind, Bohden offered his thoughts on the thin silver lining to their precarious situation. "I never thought I'd feel freer as a fugitive than I did as a citizen," he said as he stepped over a fallen log in his path, one of many they had encountered along the jagged terrain.

Lambert half smiled in response to Bohden's optimism. He knew what the friendly giant was attempting. "You'll have to explain that one a little better."

"This is the first time in my life that I'm not living for what comes next. I'm not being held hostage by the hope of those damn discharge papers. I'm not at the mercy of that viper and her damn court hearings. I'm not even worried that I've criticized the Empire . . . as crazy as that sounds."

"That's because there's nobody here to rat you out for it. I don't miss it, either. The self-policing society that ties each other in bondage," replied Lambert.

Invested in where Lambert was headed, Arlo broke his contemplative silence on the matter. "The watchful citizens' program had good intent, in my opinion. It curbed many potential crimes, even some uprisings."

"Did it, now? Maybe we should tell the Americans that," Lambert mocked.

"Yes, the irony is not lost to me," Arlo muttered.

"If you ask me, all the program did was create crimes with broad enough criteria that everyone became a suspect or a prosecutor. That's a pyrrhic victory at best."

"It was also supposed to be temporary. It was only meant to be around until Parliament shifted to the new party and the dissidents had adjusted."

"When has the Crown ever recalled anything it's implemented under the guise of being temporary?"

"Is it that wrong if it saves lives, though?"

"Hypothetically it saves lives. It can also ruin a life from mere speculation. Try operating in society after it's falsely labeled you a criminal."

In the absence of an immediate response from Arlo, Gale offered his thoughts. "Why did it take us till now to realize all this? Why did we never see it this way before?"

"It's hard to see what's been normalized until you get outside of it," concluded Lambert.

Bohden abruptly halted the team. "Hold up. We should turn north here," he said with Gideon's watch in his hand. He then further examined the digital screen to double-check his reading. "Yup, it's this way," he noted with certainty, drifting away from the group and leading the new direction.

Several steps into his adjusted course, Bohden's foot tripped a wire cable hidden within the fallen leaves that littered the ground. As the cable snapped, and the trap was sprung, a shotgun blast was fired from the trees above, scattering buckshot across the area and forcefully knocking him to the ground.

The startling boom of the gunshot sent Arlo's team desperately scrambling for cover behind the nearest trees they could find. After finding safety behind the thickest trunk, Arlo peered out to find Bohden and yelled to him, "Bohden!?"

At first there was nothing, no response. Arlo then peeked his head to see Bohden lying motionless. "Shit," Arlo said, but was then settled by Bohden reaching out and grabbing the dirt. "I'm alright!" grunted Bohden in a fractured voice as he rolled over and crawled to the cover of a tree. Resting against the jagged bark, Bohden examined the damage. The shot had mostly hit his left arm, lodging an array of buckshot pellets into the first few layers of skin. The bleeding was minimal. He told the others, "I'm good!"

Just then, Arlo saw the silhouette of a man dart across the forest and take aim at Bohden. Arlo raised his rifle and fired a small burst that disrupted the attack. "Contact, north!" Arlo shouted to the others.

With a brief window available, Lambert attempted to reposition with Lucy, but just as he did, another shotgun blast was fired from the opposite direction. "Fuckin' hell! We got two of 'em!" yelled Lambert as he dove to the ground and grabbed Lucy, dragging her with him behind cover.

Again, Arlo saw the same figure dash from behind the trees and disappear behind the obscurity of the thick forest. "Gale! Cover the south!" commanded Arlo as he leaped from cover and rushed to Bohden. Arlo fired several bursts of blind fire into the trees, hoping to keep their attacker pinned down.

Just before Arlo reached Bohden, another gunshot was fired, this time from the east, causing Arlo to dive to the ground and scramble to close the gap between him and Bohden.

"Fuckin' 'ell. We're surrounded," Bohden said,

pulling Arlo to cover behind the tree.

A voice then shouted from the woods, "You goddamn red coats should have stayed in London where you belong! You were never welcome here!"

Upon realizing the allegiance of their attacker, Arlo yelled from behind the tree he had settled into, "You got us wrong! We're not your enemy!"

"Like hell you aren't! That's a red coat flag you're wearing!" replied the man.

"No! Just give me a chance to explain!" pleaded Arlo.

"Explain what? How to lick the boot of your King!? Fuck off!"

"No! Just listen to me!" Arlo said as he attempted to emerge from cover.

Bohden grabbed him and urged him to reconsider. "Arlo, don't. That's a mad man out there."

"There's always room for diplomacy," Arlo reasoned as he set down his rifle and stepped out with his hands raised. "This is not what it looks like. We're no friends to the Crown. They're trying to kill us! That's why we're out here!"

"Prove it!"

Realizing he had little to work with, Arlo searched his options as he eyed the many potential locations of his opponents in the trees. "We got two options here. You can either take me at my word, or we can wait around for them to drop a thousand pounder on this forest. Your call."

"What are they after you for?"

"Plenty. Now either come out or let us be on our way. For both our sakes."

"Tell the others to lower their weapons!"

Arlo waved his hand, gesturing for his team to stand down. With great reluctance, both Lambert and Gale disengaged, lowering their rifles.

"Alright. They've held their end. What'll it be?"

From behind the trees emerged the source of the ambush: a single American soldier who was run ragged and weathered by the wilderness. With his weapon ready, he descended the elevated terrain and approached Arlo. The soldier's presence was tattered from a life lived in the wild, made clear by a long gray beard and aging leather bomber's jacket. He spoke with a voice that sounded as if it were coming through a blown speaker. It was hoarse and deep, but imbued with an undertone of wisdom. "So, you four are the reason these woods got flooded with Imperials?"

"Yes. Where're the rest of you?" Arlo asked, eyeing the trees.

"It's just me. . . ." The man's eyes then glanced over the emblem patch on Arlo's uniform. The embroidered white knife was familiar to him. "You're 1st group, huh? That was my old unit."

"You were Crown Special Forces?" Arlo asked.

"For all ten years under Colonel Banner. He still around?"

"He retired," said Lambert as he joined the gathering with the others.

"Never thought he would. Miserable son of a bitch. Was he still driving the red rover?"

"He was," continued Lambert.

"Huh. So where you all headed?"

"The Neutral Zone," replied Arlo.

"Not much there, I can tell you that," answered the man.

"It's better than where we were headed," said Lambert.

The man then held out his tattered, grime-covered

hand to Arlo and said, "Name's Ezra."

As Arlo grabbed and shook Ezra's hand, he told him, "Arlo. This is Lambert, Gale, and the one you shot is Bohden."

"Right. . . . Nothing personal," said Ezra as he waved his hand at Bohden, who groaned, "I'll live."

"Well, let's get him patched up. Come on," Ezra stated as he tossed his shotgun over his shoulder and turned to lead the group away.

"You have shelter?" Arlo asked before joining.

"You could call it that."

. . .

After their unusual meeting, Ezra led Arlo's team back through the forest, guiding them to a small woodland cabin built upon a subtle alpine hill. More a vacation property than a militant safehouse, Lambert was first to remark on the dissonance as his eyes scanned over the tranquil wraparound porch that hosted a breathtaking view of the majestic mountain backdrop. "Lovely getaway. . . ."

"Aye. Quite the casualty of title 70," replied Ezra.

Confused, Bohden asked Ezra, "Title 70?"

Gale interjected with an answer. "Imperial directive that came from the outbreak of the war. Allowed the Empire to seize any property for wartime use."

"But only for the duration of their activity," added Arlo.

"Which happens to be a never-ending war—though I'm not complaining. After they realized they were never going to win the wilderness, those idiots pulled their forces out of here so fast, they left behind half their armory," Ezra concluded as he stepped forward to climb the hill.

After the brief ascent, Ezra opened the front door and allowed Arlo's team to enter. They immediately noticed that the entire interior of the cabin was gutted and transformed into an improvised militant compound. Everything that would have made it a comfortable woodland getaway was missing, replaced with the elements of imperial warfare operations: supply crates, ammo boxes, munitions, and rations.

In the center of the open layout, there was an exposed living room where the ceiling reached the second story. Along the largest wall of the room, a set of windows hosted a view of the entire forest, all the way to the horizon where the sky was a soft pink from the setting sun.

After bringing his peculiar company inside, Ezra dragged out an old wooden chair for Bohden. He then crossed the room to a set of pine cabinets from which he grabbed a half full bottle of aged whiskey. "I ran out of medical supplies a while back, but I find this to be a far more useful way to numb out pain."

Intrigued by Ezra's remarks, Gale asked, "You ran out of supplies? How long have you been out here?"

"Three months," Ezra stated as he passed Bohden the bottle of amber-colored hard liquor. Just before taking a large swig, Bohden asked, "The hell you doing out here for that long?"

Ezra dodged Bohden's question, telling him "Can't say . . . not yet, at least."

"Don't trust us?" Arlo asked as he looked to continue his efforts of diplomacy.

Ezra took a casual seat upon the table beside Arlo and told him, "I'll say this much: What we have here sure as hell ain't a coincidence."

"What is it, then?" Arlo continued.

"Providence."

"I'm sorry, but I won't indulge the supernatural if that's where you're taking this."

"For claiming to be no friend to the Crown, you sure do talk like one of 'em."

"Corrupt or not, I still like to believe they may have gotten some things right."

"Would you be willing to give the Americans the same grace?"

Ezra's question prompted Arlo into a state of duality as he was forced to confront his lingering defense of the Crown. As Arlo waded through his thoughts, Ezra added, "I was in your shoes once, too. Trained to believe that the Americans were nothing more than mindless anarchists . . . but freedom for everyone doesn't mean chaos."

Reactively, Arlo brushed off Ezra's words and contested them. "You believe freedom is for everyone, but you're willing to bomb innocent civilians? What about their freedom? Where was their choice?"

Ezra shook his head with disappointment. "The fact that you believe that story is proof of what happens when you have a government that chooses what you get to see and hear."

"Are the Americans any different? You expect me to believe that they don't distort information to fit an agenda?" said Arlo.

"If we were able to, don't you think we would have done so by now? Don't you think we would have at least corrected the very lie that started this war in the first place?"

An infectious yet distressing thought occurred to Arlo. *Was the war itself another lie woven by the Empire?*

Eventually, it was Lambert who broke the silence to gain an answer. "What are you on about?" he challenged.

"All we ever wanted was the peaceful formation of an independent nation here in the colonies. Like those before us, we called it America. You may not know it, but support for the cause was overwhelming—enough so that the Crown had to acknowledge it. But when it came time for them to listen to us . . . the bombs went off. They told the world that it was us who did it, but that's what the Empire does. It attacks itself using the mask of whatever enemy it wants to turn the world against."

"Do you have any proof of this?" Lambert asked with a heavy sincerity.

"What if I did?"

"In what form?" Gale said.

"Footage, audio, pictures, you name it."

Gale shook his head in response, doubting the reality of Ezra's claim. "It would be impossible to get anything digital to the public. The Imperial surveillance network would flag it in a second and pull it."

"You underestimate us."

"Then why haven't you done anything with it?" asked Arlo.

"We were trying, but my team was shot down in transit for delivery. I was the only survivor."

"Three months is a long time to wait for search and rescue," Bohden observed.

"Yes. Believe me, you're not the only ones questioning the leadership of your army."

"If we helped you get this proof out, what are the options?" asked Lambert with a focused determination.

"You're offering help? What's the catch?"

"Let's just say I've seen enough of what the

Crown is willing to do to get what it wants. If you have proof of what you say, people deserve to see it. So, as I said, what are the options?"

"If I can reconnect with our intelligence network, they would be able to complete the mission."

"How would we do that?" Lambert continued.

"The Neutral Zone would be the best option."

"I thought you said there was nothing there?" Arlo asked, puzzled.

"That was before I knew I could get your help."

Frustrated, Arlo pressured Ezra. "Anything else we should know?"

"Transparency is something that's earned."

"Trust also works both ways, especially when you've already shot one of us," Arlo
replied.

"I have an idea. How about I show you the evidence? Maybe that will help to put all of this in perspective."

.   .   .

Nightfall had descended, and a small campfire was

started with fresh wood from Ezra's large tarp-covered supply. Chopping trees was his best method of passing the time while he waited out the grim hope of an American rescue team. The fire's flame was kept dim and low, leaving it well obscured by the surrounding forest. Crackling pine and sizzling embers were heard as the small blaze burned amongst the group of Arlo, Ezra, Lambert, and a sleeping Lucy.

Even after seeing Ezra's evidence, Arlo needed to know more about his eccentric and uncanny new ally. He started with the best point of reference he could find—life in the Imperial military. "So, what all did you do under Banner?" Arlo casually asked.

Ezra's gaze was pulled from the fire. He searched his memory to the hazy distance of his origins in Crown Special Forces. "We were assigned to Southern Africa, defending the Crown's claim on the ports. We would move from town to town and drive out the militias."

"So that's where you got your tactics?" Arlo reasoned as he connected the dots of Ezra's strategic ambush in the forest.

"You mean the remote triggers?"

"Is that what they were?"

"Yeah. There were so few of us back then and we were always outnumbered, so we came up with all kinds of ways to make the militia believe there were dozens of us. We would line the streets and alleys with remote fuses that would fire off blank rounds. It would always corral them into the choke points and force a retreat. Funny how it worked every time."

"Brilliant way to adapt," Arlo replied.

"Maybe. But I was young then; I didn't think or know better. Back then I was convinced the locals were just radicals unwilling to accept the grace of the Empire. But now, here I am. . . . God is indeed a master of irony when he wants to be."

"So, you are a believer, then?" Arlo asked.

"You say it with such condemnation."

"Well, I think rightfully so."

"And why's that?"

"The Great Correction ended one of humanity's darkest chapters. I can't imagine someone protesting its validity."

"And who taught you to think that? The same people who lied to you about everything else?"

"The Crown may have its failings, but what is

bringing God back supposed to accomplish? If that is indeed what you're advocating?"

"Making God illegal doesn't render him nonexistent."

"God is an idea, and the illegality of it has brought us unparalleled peace."

"You call what we have now peace?"

"I call it progress. We're not living our lives under superstitions or burning the innocent at the stake. Nor are we slaughtering people by the millions in the name of someone who is supposed to be benevolent."

"You just witnessed proof of the Crown bombing its own citizens and then blaming America. Is that any different than blaming God for the actions of evil men?

"This is different."

"Like hell it is."

"Do all Americans share your beliefs?" Lambert asked, refocusing the teetering conversation.

"Yes. It's fundamental. What we want most is to create a nation that is governed by God. Not by man."

"Is that really what all this has been about? God?" replied Arlo, questioning his commitment to help Ezra, given his revealed beliefs.

"You clearly hate God, but do you know who hates him even more? The Crown. And do you know why? Because God gives man absolutes. He tells us what's right and what's wrong. What's true and what's false. Do you not see what a problem that is for the Crown? The Great Correction was never about saving man from his supernatural problem; it was about erasing God, all so that the Crown could masquerade in his place, telling the world that wrong is right and lies are truth."

"I've never thought of it that way," Lambert said with clear introspection.

"Do you agree with him?" asked Arlo.

"Do I believe that people treat government like God? Absolutely."

"We ought to obey God over man," Ezra said. "If I had believed that all those years ago, I would have walked away from every order, every directive that I knew was wrong and corrupt. I wouldn't have destroyed the lives of so many people while I hid behind the lie that I was just doing my job." Ezra then stood to leave, but just before departing, he said, "It will be sunrise in a few hours. Are we gonna do this or not?"

"You'll have our answer by then," replied Arlo.

"I hope so," Ezra concluded as he left the fire and headed for the cabin.

"What do you think?" Arlo asked Lambert.

"About him, or the evidence?"

"Both, I suppose."

"He's a bit dodgy for me. Smart . . . but dodgy. However, what he showed us is irrefutable. Especially having survived an attempt of the same thing."

Arlo furrowed his brow with frustration as he replied to Lambert. "I just don't understand the need for so many lies and schemes. Why kill innocent people and blame it on your enemy?"

"Because ideas are harder to destroy than people. Seems the goal was to make the very thought of America a threat to the public."

Still too perplexed by the idea, Arlo shook off his trouble for the time being. "I suppose you're right," he said as he stood up. Looking out into the abyss-like forest and then back to the fire, he said to Lambert, "Not sure how long Gideon is going to wait around for us, especially after this much of a delay."

"Something tells me if he needs to find us, he will," Lambert said as he stretched out his legs and leaned back on his bag of equipment.

"Right. Well, get some rest."

"Believe me, I intend to."

Departing from the fire, Arlo wandered back through the house and down into the unfinished basement where Bohden appeared right at home taking inventory of the additional available gear.

Bohden turned his attention to see Arlo descending the particle board stairwell. "Evening, chief," he said as he set down a belt of grungy, copper-tipped bullets.

"Taking inventory?" Arlo asked, with a familiar manner.

"I don't know about you, but I don't have much ammo left. Figured whatever we do, we'll need a way to fight."

"I came to get your vote about joining Ezra."

"I'll say this much: The man's not bluffing. That evidence will shake the world if it gets out."

"Agreed, but there is one other thing that I feel you should consider about all this."

"And here I thought things couldn't get more complicated."

"Ezra's a believer."

Bohden raised an eyebrow and turned to Arlo. "Is he, now?"

"Yes, it's been an . . . interesting evening."

"So, is that enough for us to condemn him?"

"I'm not sure, to be honest."

"What can we be sure of anymore? Bloody up is down, the Crown's mental, the Americans aren't the enemy. Where does it end? Was anything ever honest? At this point, maybe there really is a fuckin' old chap in the sky on a throne. I don't know. . . ."

"I think the line needs to be drawn somewhere."

"So where's yours, if I may ask? . . . Respectfully."

"I'm working on that."

"Right, well, I can appreciate the warning. I guess I'll think on it."

"He wants to leave at sunrise."

Bohden nodded his head in response. As he did, Arlo noticed something in the room. "Is that an X90?" he asked at the sight of a shoulder-fired rocket launcher resting on a row of ammo crates.

"Aye, it is, and that's not all," said Bohden as he

lifted a set of night vision goggles along with a box of grenades. "Whatever we decide, we'll be all sorted out leaving here, that's for sure."

"Right. Well. Get some rest. Could be a long road ahead."

"You, too, chief."

. . .

For hours, Arlo lay awake on the hardwood floor of the living room with nothing but a tactical bag for a pillow. The attempt to rest however, was futile. His mind was unwilling to yield its racing thoughts and anxieties. His eyes were no different as they shifted all around the room.

When Arlo noticed the dim aura of dawn inching its way above the trees, he knew that it was finally time to surrender the battle for sleep. Frustrated, he got up and headed for the back porch.

Stepping through the sliding glass door, Arlo found another victim of a sleepless night, Gale. Being the intellectual loner that he was, Gale spent the night immersed in a small collection of Ezra's books. He lit the words on the pages with a reading light that was collecting a small swarm of tiny insects. Just beside him was his loaded rifle, ready to react, should the need arise.

"You look more troubled than usual," Gale mumbled to Arlo without lifting his eyes from the page of his book.

"Not sure if troubled is the word I would use," replied Arlo as he took notice of Gale's impressive stack of books. "Couldn't sleep, either?"

"Nothing new. Found some light reading instead."

"Does he know you have these?"

"I assume there was a reason he left them where he did."

"Be careful, then."

"Still don't trust him?"

"Not quite sure where I stand right now . . . he's a believer."

"Haven't heard that phrase in a while."

"What do you make of it, then?"

Gale lifted his eyes from his book. As he peered into the tree line, he took a moment to think on his response before speaking. "I think I have a question for you first."

"Yeah? What's that?"

"What does having rights mean to you? Not what you want it to mean, but what have you been told it means?"

Arlo took a moment, searching for the words he thought were best. "A right is a privilege granted by the King to his subjects."

"So a right is given to someone from their government?"

"I would agree with that, yes."

In response, Gale proceeded to read from his book: "We hold these truths to be self-evident, that all men are created equal, that they are endowed by their Creator with certain unalienable Rights, that among these are Life, Liberty, and the pursuit of Happiness. That to secure these rights, Governments are instituted among Men, deriving their just powers from the consent of the governed—That whenever any Form of Government becomes destructive of these ends, it is the Right of the People to alter or to abolish it, and to institute new Government, laying its foundation on such principles."

Arlo's posture changed. He crossed his arms and became guarded, yet his face could not help but hint that he was curious. "What's that from?" he said hesitantly.

"The Declaration of Independence for a United States of America. This is what the original Americans drafted for King George when they decided to separate from the Crown."

"You sure that's not a forgery?"

"Can't tell. But I'm of the opinion that most of what the Crown has told us is an outright lie, anyways . . . especially after seeing the evidence Ezra showed us."

Arlo then voiced a thought that was circling his mind. "When they say creator, do they mean—"

"God. Yes. In their view, we are created beings designed with intent to fulfill a purpose, and that purpose requires freedom. Which is why he's a believer. This can't work unless rights themselves derive from our origin, from God, not from our so-called rulers. 'Least that's what this proposes."

"You've really opened up to this, haven't you?"

"All I can say is that I like the idea of having been born with the right to be free. It gives life a certain majesty."

"So, then your vote is to help him?"

"What other choice do we really have?"

CHAPTER 7

At sunrise, Ezra stood in front of the house, waiting for Arlo and his men to emerge. The forest was still and silent, and a low mist was resting just above the ground, mirroring the veil of uncertainty about the journey ahead.

As the minutes passed, so did Ezra's fragile hope for Arlo and his team. Doubtful ruminations were settling in. *Was the evidence not convincing enough?* he thought. Or was it the revelation of his beliefs? Had it sabotaged the last chance he may have to make use of what so many American lives had worked to obtain?

Assuming the worst, he leaned down to grab a worn leather bag and slung it over his shoulder. As he secured the pack, he heard the front door open. His eyes snapped to see Lambert with Lucy close by his side. Just behind was Gale, dressed and equipped for the operation. As both men descended the front steps of the porch, Lambert pointed behind him and said, "Bohden is grabbing the last of the supplies from the basement; he'll be right out."

Looking past them and into the house, Ezra asked, "What did Arlo decide?"

"Don't know. Haven't seen him yet," Lambert replied as he joined the group.

After the porch door slammed shut behind him, Bohden emerged carrying two bags of rifles, ammo, and assorted gear. He balanced the heavy weight of the bags until he tossed them at everyone's feet. "Every man should at least take a backup rifle and some ammo," he advised as he opened the rugged canvas bags.

Then the sound of crackling branches and snapping twigs gripped everyone's attention; it was Arlo emerging from behind the bushes. As he approached the startled group, he told them, "No sign of the Empire, or anyone for at least a couple miles on the path."

"Did you sleep, chief?" asked Bohden in a concerned tone.

"No. Figured I would scout out instead."

Confused by Arlo's actions, Lambert asked, "You've been out here all night?"

"What was left of it. Assuming nothing goes

wrong, it's still half a day's hike from here to the border." Arlo then looked to Bohden, asking, "Does the GPS still have our path?"

"Aye. It does," Bohden confirmed as he looked upon the illuminated digital trail to the Neutral Zone.

"Is that the path you mentioned? Can I see it?" asked Ezra as he leaned in to glimpse Gideon's watch.

"Sure," said Bohden, giving the device to Ezra.

Quickly scanning it, he told the group, "This takes us through the farmlands. That's Imperial jurisdiction. Who told you to go this way?"

Arlo eyed his teammates, letting them know what he was about to reveal. "Let me ask you this instead. Do the Americans have stealth technology?"

"Like radar, or what?" Ezra replied.

"No. Optical camouflage, turns the user invisible. Can't even see or hear them move," answered Arlo.

"This would be a much different fight if we had something like that."

"If that's the case, then we should trust what this says," Arlo concluded as he took Gideon's watch back from Ezra.

"Whoever gave you this is either foolish or

sending you into a trap," Ezra said.

Gale shook his head, informing Ezra, "Unlikely. Not after what we've been through."

"Which is what?"

"Transparency is earned, no?" said Arlo.

"Which I've given you."

Lambert stepped forward to ask, "Is there a better way to the Neutral Zone, then?"

"Yes, we follow the mountains. The woods will cover us the whole way," Ezra replied, pointing to the distant forest beyond the horizon.

"So you want us to believe that you've known the way there this entire time, but you've just camped out here, hoping for rescue? Forgive me, but that doesn't add up," said Lambert.

Ezra was stricken to silence as he realized he was backed into a corner that he refused to explain himself out of. As Lambert realized this, he told Ezra, "Looks like we're not the only ones keeping secrets here."

Frustrated and impatient, Arlo broke the stalemate. "We're on the run from the Crown because one of our own lied to us to get us to accept this mission, trapped us in a barn and torched it." Arlo then lifted

Gideon's watch and said, "The man who gave us this pulled us from that fire, told us the truth, and proved it. Right now, our deaths, which will be blamed on the Americans, are being exploited all over London to justify restarting this war. . . . Your turn."

"I . . ." mumbled Ezra as he trailed into silence, still unwilling to give his reasons.

"If your goal is truly to vindicate your people and expose the lies, then your best option is with us because that's where I'm leading this. No matter what," Arlo said, then turned and departed for the path. His team followed just behind him, leaving Ezra alone to make his choice.

As he watched Arlo and his men enter the trees and begin the journey without him, Ezra looked up through the forest, peering into the sliver of sky. He lingered with his indecision for only a moment more. With a firm grip on his bag, Ezra stepped forward to rejoin the team.

.   .   .

The first length of the hike was a hot, damp, six-hour trek down from the elevated terrain of Ezra's cabin. Gideon's path led the team of five in a descent to the base of the mountains where the density of trees thinned and yielded.

After almost two days of unrelenting struggle, each man's appearance reflected everything that transpired since the leap from the drop plane. Every inch of fabric, kit, and skin was layered with jagged streaks of dirt, grime, blood, and soot. Their exhausted eyes were injected with red from trauma, stress, and sleeplessness.

Upon arriving at the vast foothills of the mountain, the team could see a wide valley of smooth, level fields hosting infinite acreage of grassy meadows.

As they came upon the new terrain, they entered a pasture of tall grass calmly flowing in what seemed like an ethereal wind. The view was an unbroken canvas of vibrant greens and deep yellows, a welcome break from the never-ending claustrophobia of the forest.

Lambert was the first to step into the open expanse. As the waist-high grass brushed against him, he held out his tattered hand to feel it. Turning back to see the others emerge from the veil of the forest, he asked, "Bohden, is this where we turn northeast?"

"Aye! We cross this valley and then the border is beyond that range," Bohden replied, referencing Gideon's device.

After Gale stepped into the field, his curious eyes took in the setting, prompting him to ask Ezra, "I was reading last night that the original militia from the 1700s fought in these same fields?"

Perplexed by the revealing of Gale's knowledge, Ezra asked, "You read my books?"

"As many as I could, yes."

Puzzled but impressed all the same, Ezra told Gale, "The fighting did eventually spill over into these fields, but the initial outbreak of the war took place more to the southeast. Back then it was called Lexington. Two of the original American philosophers, Sam Adams and John Hancock, were hiding there and avoiding arrest."

Gale then probed further. "Sam Adams, he helped author the declaration for independence, right?"

"More than that, he helped author both declarations—the one for independence and the one for natural rights."

"Why two separate documents?" Gale asked.

"The Declaration of Rights was an evolution of the American movement. It was the enumeration of natural rights that the American government would be bound to uphold."

Arlo's interest was piqued. He asked Ezra, "What rights were enumerated?"

"Well, the first was, and I quote, that there shall be no law respecting an establishment of religion, or prohibiting the free exercise thereof; or abridging the freedom of speech, or of the press; or the right of the people peaceably to assemble, and to petition the Government for a redress of grievances."

Ezra's words pulled Lambert back into the discussion. "Freedom of speech huh? So, in your world, I could speak openly against the Crown and, what? Not be locked up?"

"Exactly, if you can't criticize corruption, then how can it ever be addressed?"

"What if the people criticized a good government? What happens if someone misleads others into sabotaging something that is good?" Arlo asked.

"I think you assume that the vision of America was a democracy. It wasn't. Democracy is the fastest path to what you just mentioned—mob rule."

Arlo continued, "What was America supposed to be, then?"

"A Republic. Governance by law, which is directly opposed to that of a democracy, which is governance by popular opinion. In a republic, laws are written to protect and uphold fundamental truths of humanity like rights, liberty, prosperity, things that don't change. Democracies allow special interests to exploit the opinions of the masses and lead to the creation of the mob that destroys its own way of life, which is what's happened every time Democracy has been tried."

"Interesting . . . were the other rights as radical?" asked Arlo.

"Depends on how you define radical."

"Private gun ownership might be considered radical," said Gale, offering his insight on the matter.

Confused and overwhelmed by the thought, Arlo winced and said, "Fuckin' 'ell, are you serious?"

Ezra took the chance to explain. "Yes. They wanted citizens to be able to preserve their nation from any enemy, foreign . . . or domestic. How can a citizen double as a soldier without arms?"

"Soldiers should be ordained by governments."

"And if the government becomes wicked and corrupt, like all have? What then?"

"Regardless of a corrupt government, what would happen if criminals armed themselves and turned violent on the citizens?"

"Then the criminals are a domestic enemy to the prosperity of the nation, are they not? And thankfully, the citizens would be armed with the means to defend themselves against those criminals. The opposite happens every day where you're from, even without guns. How many senseless murders take place on the streets of London because citizens are helpless? Their only option is to hope that their life matters enough for the Crown to do something about it. Which in most cases, it doesn't. And at the end of the day, there is no reason for a government to fear an armed populace, unless the government intends to do something that the populace would need to defend itself from."

"I just don't know if I agree with everything you're saying," Arlo stated reluctantly.

"Only because you were trained to believe that the government exists to protect the government, not the rights of its people."

"And if my opinion is against yours, then am I a member of the mob that must be opposed?"

Frustrated, Ezra came to a stop amidst the field. He turned, confronting Arlo. "I think at this point, if you don't believe in the idea of America, why are you helping us?"

"Because I believe in correcting injustice, which I've been convinced is the case with this war."

"Then do you actually believe that there was a motive to that injustice? If America is foolish and senseless, then why lie to the entire world to prevent them from learning about it? . . . Twice."

Arlo desperately searched his thoughts for a rebuttal, but his mental scramble was interrupted by an approaching helicopter from just over the mountain.

"I told you this was Imperial territory!" said Ezra as he searched the sky for the helicopter.

Worried that the chopper was searching the area for the team, Arlo directed everyone to scatter and hide. The sudden adrenaline rush sent each man sprinting to conceal themselves from view. Arlo, Gale, and Ezra ran back into the forest and ducked behind the largest trees they could find. Bohden, Lambert, and Lucy scrambled to a massive fallen pine log that they hid beneath.

Within moments, the roaring thunder of the

helicopter shook the air like a drumhead. Arlo's mind raced at the sound of it; he knew that every Imperial aircraft had thermal imaging, and if Gideon's scrambler was not holding, then they would stand out on the monitors. He peeked up through the canopy to determine the direction that the aircraft was coming. As he did, the dark silhouette of the helicopter soared across the sky and away from the group. After it passed the forest line, it continued down the valley.

Once the forceful sound faded to a safe distance, each man stepped out from hiding. Looking out toward the horizon, Bohden said to everyone as they came back together, "That was lucky."

"Agreed, but do you hear that? Sounds like it's landing," replied Gale.

"Could be deploying a search party," Lambert offered.

Gale agreed, and advised, "We should find out what we're dealing with, then adjust accordingly."

"Either way, the path takes us right to 'em," Bohden said, checking coordinates from the GPS.

.　　.　　.

As the helicopter continued across the verdurous plains of the valley, it headed for a congenial farm and homestead located some miles ahead of the aircraft's path. The property itself was a bastion of seclusion, a fragile retreat from the looming nightmare of war taking place all around it. One could imagine the infinite memories of youthful human splendor that had taken place within its natural walls. This impression was about to end as the Imperial rotor wing came in for an unwelcomed landing.

The violent noise of the helicopter was something so unfamiliar to the area that it drew out the owners of the property, an old gray-bearded farmer named Jeremiah and his wife, Anne.

As Jeremiah's stoic gaze followed the helicopter in, Anne said to him with nervousness in her voice, "What would the Empire be doing all the way out here? They've never come this far north."

"I don't know . . . but I want you to stay inside. I'll deal with them," Jeremiah said, and stepped down the porch staircase, traversing the dirt road that led to the small farm fields surrounding the house. He arrived just in time to be buffeted by the winds of the rotor blades as the aircraft finally landed.

With the helicopter holding at idle, a squadron of faceless Legion troopers disembarked and marched into a formation beside the aircraft. They stood with robotic posture, awaiting their commander to direct them further. Once the eighth and final trooper was deployed, Lieutenant Blackburn stepped out from the cabin. Blackburn, much like Captain Wallcroft before him, was the next officer in line to conduct Sheridan's orders. His appearance all together was the same—ruthless and regal.

With every Imperial now unloaded, the behemoth troop transport took flight and headed back to the nearest base to refuel and carry on the war effort.

Jeremiah stood between his home and the ominous squadron marching toward him like an enveloping shadow. Blackburn's long black cape tossed about in the wind and contrasted the seamless and synchronous steps of each soldier. Closing the distance, Blackburn and his men came to a stop some twenty yards from the house.

At first, Blackburn said nothing. His eyes scanned to take in the area, eventually falling upon Jeremiah's defensive glare. Blackburn's lust for authority and dominance was contested by the weathered farmer's unmoved stone figure and stable eyes. "You may address me as Lieutenant Blackburn," the officer said, after a long, uneasy silence.

"What can I do for you, then . . . Lieutenant?"

"By order of the King, your property has been chosen to be our staging area for reconnaissance. We are to be provided housing and hospitality for the duration of our mission."

"I was under the impression that troop quartering was only allowed during a state of war?"

"Are you attempting to feign ignorance, or take me as a fool?"

"Neither. Respectfully, I'm just wondering what you're really doing here since, as you can see
. . . there's no war here."

"On the contrary, there has been an unusual amount of American activity in this area. Which I assume you know nothing about?"

"No. We moved here to get away from that mess."

"Very well. However, your property still falls within the realm of Imperial territory. Therefore the mandate still applies."

"Seems I don't have much of a choice. I guess you and your men are welcome. I'll have my wife prep the rooms."

"First, we will be conducting a search of the premises."

Blackburn's reaching demand finally provoked a reaction from Jeremiah's guarded posture, his brow raised ever so slightly as he asked, "For what reason?"

"Should it matter, if you have nothing to hide?"

"Since when does paranoia justify suspicion?"

Blackburn half smiled as he waved his soldiers forward to conduct the search. After they tore open the front door and entered the house, Blackburn said to Jeremiah, "If there's something you wish to confess, then perhaps I will consider granting you mercy."

The sound of the front door slamming shut prompted both men to turn and notice two of Blackburn's soldiers emerging from the house with several firearms, an old shotgun, and a bolt-action rifle. One of the Imperial soldiers presented his findings to Blackburn like a hunting hound carrying a dead fox.

"Oh, my. What have we here?" sneered

Blackburn with a ruthless smirk.

"I don't know what works for you all in the city, but out here, things are different. Am I not allowed to protect myself?"

"If it's protection you require, then you are to request the nearest agent of the Crown for the matter."

"The nearest town is almost a hundred miles. . . ."

"Your choice to live at such a distance is not a justification for the high crime of owning a deadly weapon."

"Self-defense is not a crime."

"Under whose law? Yours?"

"There was also this, sir," one of the soldiers added as he handed Blackburn a leather-bound book engraved with a golden cross on the cover.

"My, my, and not a moment ago you attempted to lecture me on the futility of suspicion. Ready arms!"

At Blackburn's order, his soldiers snapped their weapons up, aiming for a swift execution. "Renounce your superstitions or suffer the consequence."

"I will not," said Jeremiah.

"Seems you are intent on forcing my hand. Fi—" But before Blackburn could finish his order, a thundering shotgun blast erupted from the porch and collided with an Imperial soldier, throwing him to the ground, a massive trail of blood spewing from his throat. From the porch, Anne lowered the smoking barrel of an old shotgun. She then realized the soldiers were about to return fire, prompting her to take off and sprint away.

As Anne raced across the wraparound porch, Blackburn shouted, "Open fire!"

A barrage of gunfire was unleashed into the immaculate white wood of the house, shredding and tearing apart the structure. Explosions of fractured wood and shrapnel erupted behind Anne as the gunfire chased her all the way to the other side of the house, where she was able to dive off the porch and land behind the cover of its concrete foundation.

With the Imperials distracted, Jeremiah was afforded the chance to retreat behind a large red tractor parked no more than ten feet from him. He then ripped off a large section of his shirt and unscrewed the tractor's fuel cap. Shoving the loose fabric inside, he set it ablaze with a steel frame lighter from his pocket.

Once the torn shirt began burning, Jeremiah ran toward his house. Just after vaulting across the picket fence line, the fire entered the gas tank and detonated the tractor, consuming the area in a kinetic eruption of pressure, fire, and shattered pieces of the tractor frame.

The impact of the explosion was enough to disrupt the Imperial soldiers, who dove to the ground as they tried to avoid the blast wave. Blackburn, however, was hit in the shoulder with a small chunk of shrapnel.

"Bloody scum," he grunted, gripping his bleeding arm and dislodging a rusty metal fragment. He winced and clenched his jaw, shouting to his soldiers, "What are you all standing around for!? Kill them! . . . And someone get that chopper back here!"

Jeremiah's stunt allowed him to cross the backyard of the house where he was able to reunite with wife, who was still ducking behind the cover of the foundation. Anne was locked in a frantic state, her hands trembling and still struggling to reload her shotgun. In a stuttering, panicked voice, she said, "I . . . I . . . wasn't going . . . to . . . to let them just kill you. . . ."

"It's okay. You did the right thing, but we need to get to the barn. Come on," Jeremiah urged as he took the shotgun from her and pulled her up from the dirt. As they raced across the yard, Jeremiah reloaded the shotgun, tossing out the spent shell and replacing it with a fresh cartridge. Once the round set into the firing tube, he closed the barrel and fired upon the pursuing Imperials, giving cover for Anne to enter the obscurity of the cornfield that stretched all the way to the barn.

Jeremiah was only a few steps behind his wife before another barrage of erratic gunfire began to rip into the field. "Just keep running!" Jeremiah shouted with all the force his strained lungs could gather.

After the third wave of sonic cracks sounded from the distance, Jeremiah saw a plume of red mist burst from his wife's back. She tumbled forward and into the ground.

"No! No! No!" pleaded Jeremiah as he dropped the shotgun and dashed ahead to lift Anne's body.

Crossing the short distance to the barn, he ran through the large sliding door at the front. Trailing just behind him, fitful gunfire slammed into the walls of the barn. Once Jeremiah was out of view, Blackburn commanded his men to cease fire and press forward.

At the other end of the barn, there was an old hay-covered pickup truck that Jeremiah hoped might still work. Before searching for the keys, he ran to the back and pulled down the tailgate, gently setting Anne upon the rusted truck bed.

As he ripped her shirt to expose the wound, Jeremiah could see that the bullet had gone all the way through and exited the front, near her stomach, creating a catastrophic stream of blood that now covered his hands and arms.

Knowing she had only moments left, Anne grabbed her husband's hand, pleading, "You can still make it if you run. . . ."

"No, no, you're gonna be okay. . . ." he replied, believing the lie he was telling himself.

"You have to get out of here and warn the children. Don't let them come back here." Anne's breaths then become shallow and further apart. "Anne . . . stay with me . . . please," wept Jeremiah with a choking voice and watering eyes.

"I love you," she said in a near whisper before dying in Jeremiah's arms.

Realizing she was gone, he tried lifting her, but his knees buckled, causing him to fall to the ground with her body held close. He then lost himself to an agony he had never known as his stone manner shattered in a sudden rush of sobbing. As he rocked back and forth, he began to sink into the hopeless delusion that it was a nightmare, and nothing more.

.   .   .

Some distance from the farmstead, Gale was following Blackburn with the crosshairs of his rifle scope. He tracked the officer and his soldiers as they spread out to surround the barn.

Once Gale gathered the situation, he lowered his rifle and crept out of the tall grass that concealed him. As he emerged from the wall of foliage, he rejoined the others, who were gathered behind an abandoned rusted tractor. Gale took a knee among the group and told them, "They got one officer, and seven Legion troopers."

Arlo shook his head with doubt. "What the fuck happened?"

"I didn't see what started it, but they're moving on the barn. I assume the family is inside," said Gale as he then nervously looked over his shoulder and back toward the farmstead.

"We could pick 'em off from a distance if we

coordinate," Lambert offered, but was refuted when Arlo told him, "No, that'll just provoke Sheridan. He'll scramble the whole battalion to this area."

"So, then we just leave 'em to be executed?" Lambert replied.

Arlo hesitated, searching for the right choice. He then turned to Ezra. "Thoughts?"

"This isn't our fight. If they knew our mission, they would understand."

"Then you all can continue with the mission; I'm not leaving these people to die because of us." Lambert broke off from the others and headed toward the farm. Not a second later, Arlo chased him down and grabbed him by the shoulder. "What are you doing, Lambert!?"

"What are *you* doing, Arlo!? Standing idle while innocent people get executed?"

"What's going on down there is their problem. Not ours."

"Really? Then why else would the Empire even be here, if not for us?"

The argument was then abruptly cut off by the sudden return of the Imperial helicopter.

"Shit! Get down!" shouted Arlo, who grabbed

Lambert and dove with him into the grass.

As they fell into the field, they watched the aircraft pass over and circle the property like a carrion bird above wounded prey. "We can't just look the other way anymore, Arlo," said Lambert with conviction as he stared down his partner.

Completing a final pass of the property, the Imperial rotor wing settled above the cornfield. Inside the open cabin of the aircraft, two marksmen took aim with precision rifles. Each soldier panned their crosshairs to the main door of the barn, ready to engage at Blackburn's orders.

With a restored confidence in his position, Blackburn stepped forward to yell at Jeremiah, who was still sheltered in the barn. "Allow me to demonstrate for you the grace of the Empire. Surrender yourself to justice, and I will see to it personally that you be given a chance to plead your case to courts." Blackburn waited a moment for a response. He then told his soldiers, "Just think of the message it will send." With no response from Jeremiah, Blackburn raised his voice again, yelling, "You test my patience!"

Just as Blackburn was about to lose his patience

entirely, the front door of the barn opened to reveal Jeremiah.

"Keep your hands where we can see them!" shouted Blackburn as Jeremiah took several steps forward. "Go, detain him," ordered Blackburn.

Jeremiah remained still as three of the Imperials began their approach. What was not obvious to them, however, was the silver revolver Jeremiah had stashed at the back of his waistband.

With their rifles aimed and ready, the Imperials took slow and deliberate steps, cautious and ready for their captive should he try anything.

Jeremiah then witnessed a fireball shoot out from the tree line and rip across the field as fast as a lightning strike. The dazzling flare made a direct impact with the helicopter and consumed the rotor shaft in a plume of fire and ruptured metal. As it came undone, the swirling blades collapsed inward and tore apart the body of the aircraft like a buzz saw through tin foil.

It took less than a second for the entire helicopter to spiral down and crash. Upon impact, the momentum that remained within the rotors chewed and sliced the dirt, pulling the wreckage forward until finally the crash settled beneath a falling cloud of debris. A leaking gas tank then reached the fires of the wreckage. The flame took to the gas, raced up the spilling fluid, and traveled into the giant tank filled with fresh fuel. A colossal detonation followed.

As the explosive force rushed out, everyone was blown to the ground in shock. Blackburn was hit with such momentum that he was unable to stand back up. In his concussive daze, he turned to see Jeremiah crawling away to hide behind a tractor trailer near the barn. He then became bewitched by the sight of a soldier walking from the wreckage, engulfed by a fuel fire that covered his entire body.

Upon realizing that their commander was lost in delirium, one of the Imperials ran to help Blackburn up. As soon as the soldier extended his hand in aid, a gunshot ripped through his chest and sprayed blood all over Blackburn, who was finally yanked from hypnosis. All around him, his men were shouting over the sudden wave of gunfire from beyond the farmstead. "Contact! Contact! Eleven o'clock! Four o'clock!" they shouted to each other in panicked confusion.

Arlo and his team concealed themselves well

enough in the fields that no Imperial soldier could find where the gunshots were coming from.

"Bohden! Talk to me!" said Lambert amidst the bedlam of scattered gunfire.

From inside the cover of the weeds, Bohden could see that the Imperials had grabbed Blackburn and were making a run for the field beside the house. "They're making a break for the south field!" he yelled back.

"Copy! Engaging!" said Lambert. To get a better shot, Lambert stood up just slightly above the cover of the tall grass. He raised his rifle, took aim, tracked his target, and fired two precise shots into an Imperial soldier. Blackburn's men fired blindly in response, but Lambert had already ducked back down and was hidden in the grass.

During the chaos of the crash, Gale snuck through the fields to flank the fight. Once in position, he readied his rifle and toggled his scope to see Blackburn cowering on the ground. Around him, his men were standing and engaging their hidden enemy. At every break in the gunfire Blackburn would shout futile orders with escalating fury, hoping somehow that his intensity would translate to a miracle that could get them to safety.

Gale then panned his scope to see Jeremiah still hiding behind the trailer. He could tell that the anguished farmer was fixed with a bloodlust for Blackburn. At every chance he could, Jeremiah would peek around the corner and look for the officer.

Gale then zoomed his scope to see Jeremiah pull out his revolver from the concealment of his clothes. This happened just as Blackburn realized his only hope to survive the fight was to make a retreat to the woods.

As a final order to the remaining soldiers, Blackburn commanded them to hold their ground and cover his retreat. Once the order was given, Blackburn seized the opportunity by sprinting away from the gunfight. The two remaining soldiers opened fire in all directions of the field.

Just as Blackburn took off, Gale tracked him with a gradual lead in his crosshairs. Once he was confident in the placement, he fired, but the shot missed and tore through the wooden fence behind his target. Gale rapidly yanked back the bolt of his rifle and chambered another round, but it was too late. Blackburn disappeared behind the house.

Before Gale could reposition, he saw Jeremiah

take off in frantic pursuit of Blackburn. Blinded by his need for vengeance, he chased the officer without concern for the remaining soldiers who acquired him. They immediately turned and fired, but not before Gale fired first.

The well-placed shot from Gale ripped with a sonic whistle into the Imperial soldier, startling both Jeremiah and the last surviving Imperial. Jeremiah then leaned and raised his revolver, firing two shots that allowed him to escape and continue his pursuit.

Blackburn's formal attire of regal fabric and leather boots kept him at a slow, dragging pace. His hobbling caused enough delay to allow Jeremiah to catch him in gun range.

A stray, desperate gunshot landed to the right of Blackburn. As it tore up the grass beside him, he stopped and raised his hands in the air. Cautiously, he turned around to face Jeremiah.

With his revolver held tight at his hip, Jeremiah slowly entered the tall grass field and approached Blackburn with a vigilant posture. Tears of rage and loss began to seep from his eyes as he yelled, "You've taken everything from me! And for what!? Is the world safer now!? Is it more secure now that you've murdered my wife!? We were innocent! Both of us! All I wanted was to live here in peace. That's all I wanted!"

Jeremiah held back another wave of grief-stricken tears.

"Then you should have obeyed. You should have confessed when I gave you the choice."

"You never gave me a fuckin' choice for anything!"

"I am not to blame. Your only job was to submit to your King. Had you done that, your wife would still be alive." Blackburn's words were enough to collapse Jeremiah's search for an answer, but before he could pull the trigger, Blackburn drew a pistol from his hip and fired. The round tore into Jeremiah's stomach, but rather than collapse, the farmer fired, one, two, and then finally a third shot, killing Blackburn instantly.

For a moment, Jeremiah waited. With his finger still on the trigger, he searched the grass for any sign of movement. When the field settled, he finally collapsed to one knee. As he pressed a hand into the gushing wound near his liver, he heard rushing footsteps approaching. It was Gale and Bohden.

"No, no, just stay still," Bohden said, urging the farmer not to get up.

"Who the hell are you people?" Jeremiah asked with shallow, labored breathing as Bohden gently laid the farmer onto the ground.

"Ignore the uniforms, it's complicated," Bohden assured Jeremiah as best he could while he inspected his wound.

"We're with the Americans," added Gale, who drew a look of confusion from Bohden.

"I can't breathe. . . ." whispered Jeremiah in a near-hollow voice.

Immediately, Bohden eased the worry, telling him, "You're gonna be fine. I just need you to stay still for me."

Bohden ripped open his medical kit and pulled everything he needed. Once his supplies were laid out, Bohden grabbed a set of trauma shears and cut into Jeremiah's blood-soaked flannel shirt. With the wound exposed and in full view, Gale watched as the hope was ripped from Bohden's face. "Shit. . . ." he said at the sight of the wound. He then said to Gale, "Lower-right pocket there's a decompression needle. Get it now."

Prompted by the order, Gale shifted through the medical bag until he found a clear tube that encased a large needle. He tore it out of the crackling plastic cover and quickly handed it off to Bohden, who was feeling for the gap in Jeremiah's ribs. Once the space was found, he plunged the needle in and opened the valve, allowing for the compressed air and trapped blood to evacuate.

With Jeremiah's breathing stabilized, Bohden shifted his focus to the gunshot wound, which was still streaming blood. With focused hands, he tore open several gauze packages and then pressed the cloth against the gushing puncture, drenching the white cloth a deep red.

Near the front of the house, Lambert and Lucy were checking the bodies of the Imperial soldiers. As Lambert paced the corpses, Lucy did the same. Not long after they started their assessment, Arlo approached, clearly frustrated, saying, "A reaction force will be here any minute; we need to recover what we can use and keep moving."

"What about them?" Lambert said, pointing to Gale and Bohden across the way.

"We should have never come here. We should

have never intervened."

"It was the right thing to try."

"And now his wife is dead, and who the fuck knows about him. So, what did we accomplish? Wasted ammo, exposed our position?"

"That's not what this was about."

"I get it that I fucked up. I get it that I led us into this shit, but I've also held this team together through everything. I know it's a lot to ask now, but I can lead us through this . . . but not if I don't have you with me."

Several startling barks then came from Lucy, who was set off by the sight of something in the distance. Over and over, she yelped with an aggressive tone until Lambert calmed her and quickly traced the source of her concern to an old red truck approaching the farm. "Shit. What now?" said Lambert.

Traversing the long dirt road that led to the farmhouse, the diesel-chugging pickup stopped some fifty yards from the property. Once the truck was parked, a late-teens boy named Pearson stepped out and onto the loose gravel. Upon taking in the chaos, he quickly gestured for his younger sister in the passenger seat to stay put. "Wait here, Eliza," he commanded with worry clear in his voice.

As Pearson stepped forward, he saw Lambert approaching him with a militant posture. At the sight of the rifle, he became rigid and guarded.

"Turn around! Get out of here!" shouted Lambert.

"This is my home! What are you doing here!? Where are my parents!?"

The boy's words hit Lambert's heart to a near stop. "Bloody 'ell," he muttered under his breath.

"What happened!? Why are you here!?"

Lambert could tell that Pearson was about to break from the panic and confusion. The frailty in his voice was a giveaway, as were the unstable movements of his body as he fought the urge to run toward the house.

"Just stay where you are, alright? It's not safe over there," said Lambert, changing his tone to try and calm Pearson.

"Where are my parents!?"

"We are still trying to contain the situation; just remain where you are."

"Who are you!?"

Before Lambert could answer, Pearson saw Bohden and Gale carrying Jeremiah across the porch and toward the front of his house. It took only a moment for him to recognize his father's body as it drooped in Bohden's arms. "Dad!?" he cried as he charged toward the house.

Before he could make it far, Lambert leaped forward to grab Pearson and restrain him. The traumatized boy fought and screamed, forcing Lambert to grip him tighter and hold his arms as they swung and fought to break free. "Let me go, you fucking asshole! That's my dad!"

"No, kid. There's nothing for you over there. Trust me."

The anger and rage then gave way to surrender and tears as Pearson ran out of strength, "Why? Why won't you let me go?" he said, sobbing.

As Lambert continued to contain the panic, he looked up to see that Pearson's sister was motionless in the passenger seat of the truck. Her face was blank and vacant from shock.

Inside the house, Bohden and Gale carried Jeremiah down the debris-filled hallway. Their boots crushed loose glass and wood fragments as they walked to the bedroom where they laid Jeremiah down. "Easy,

easy," Bohden cautioned as they gently settled Jeremiah into place on the bed. "Stay with him," added Bohden before he stepped out to inform Arlo of the situation.

When Bohden emerged from the house, he found Arlo impatiently waiting with Ezra on the porch. "Where's Gale?" Arlo asked.

"Inside with the old man."

"How bad is it?" Ezra asked.

"Done all I can. But he's gonna bleed out."

"Does he know that?" Arlo said as he tried to comprehend the situation.

"Yeah, he knows. Who are they?" Bohden said at the sight of Lambert holding back Pearson.

"His son and daughter, who we need to hand this over to. We should have been out of here already."

"You want to just leave them for Sheridan!?" said, Bohden, stricken by Arlo's detachment.

"They'll have a better chance if it's just them. If we stay, they'll be executed alongside us," Arlo replied.

"He's right," added Ezra.

"Those Imperials were here for us. Not this family. We owe them something," demanded Bohden.

"This was inevitable. The war was eventually

going to find its way here. It's a miracle it didn't happen sooner," Ezra reasoned.

"No. We've got options! We can set up positions! Rig an ambush!"

Bohden's optimism was struck down by Arlo telling him, "We can't win a stand up with what's coming, and we've wasted enough time debating this."

Lambert's voice then suddenly broke up the meeting. "Eyes up! We got incoming!" he shouted from across the way.

Arlo ran down from the porch to get a glimpse at the horizon where Lambert acquired a single helicopter that was on approach to the property. "Goddamnit! Get them inside!" commanded Arlo as he readied to engage the incoming threat.

"What now? What's happening?" Pearson stammered as Lambert yanked him up.

"Just get your sister and follow me. Now!" ordered Lambert, prompting Pearson to shake off his fright and grab Eliza, who was still drowning in shock. He lifted his frozen sister, then held her close and followed Lambert's urgent pace to the hopeful shelter of the house.

After everyone was inside, Arlo moved to hide himself in the tall grass of the field just beside the porch. As the helicopter came closer, he loaded his rifle with a new magazine and readied to engage. Before he could, however, Ezra emerged, waving his arms, urging Arlo to stand down. "Stop! That's not the Empire!" he shouted.

By the time Ezra said this, the aircraft was close enough for Arlo to see that it was indeed different. The painting and the markings were informal, as was the ragged camouflage coating. The helicopter then banked into a wide orbit of the farm. After the pass was complete, it came around to the front where Arlo could see that there was a non-Imperial soldier riding in the back.

The aircraft lowered for landing. Its unique appearance became easier for Arlo to resolve. The entire frame and cabin were used and weathered. Multiple bullet holes and dents covered its body, and its bolts and fasteners were exposed beneath frayed paint. What intrigued Arlo the most was the eroded thirteen-star American flag painted on the side.

The landing complete, the soldier onboard leaped out and, as he emerged through the wall of dust, he approached Arlo and Ezra. "You guys have every Imperial asset in the area converging on this location. We came to see what the deal was. Name's Troy."

"Ezra. We're with the Culper ring," he stated with a matter-of-fact demeanor.

"You're with intelligence? What the hell are you doing out here, then?" continued Troy.

"Are you able to get us to the border?" Ezra asked.

"Is it just you two?"

"How many will the aircraft hold?" inquired Arlo.

"Why? How many are here?"

"Seven of us," Arlo responded hesitantly.

"Did you say seven!?"

"Yes. I'll explain later," Arlo replied.

"Fuck it. Bring 'em, but hurry. We got about ten minutes before this place is overrun."

At Troy's request, Arlo ran back to the house to gather everyone. Lambert and Gale looked at Arlo with puzzled faces as he approached them.

"That bird is with the Americans. They can pull us out. Get onboard," Arlo said as he continued past them and into the house.

Quickly crossing the hallway, Arlo came to the last bedroom, where he found Jeremiah spending his final moments with his children. Quietly, he signaled for Bohden to speak with him.

Together in the war-torn hallway, Arlo told Bohden in a quiet voice, "An American bird is here to pull us out. We can bring the kids if you can convince them to come. But you need to do it now."

"What? Where did it come from!?"

"You heard me, Bohden. Just go."

Bohden returned to the bedroom where the situation was increasingly delicate.

"You two don't need to worry about me," said Jeremiah as he took his youngest by the hand, telling her, "It's okay, Eliza, I'm going to be fine."

"I don't understand. . . . What happened?" asked Pearson.

"Your mother and I should have known that we couldn't hide from the war forever. We thought living out here would keep you safe. I'm sorry," Jeremiah said, then turned to Bohden, asking him, "Will you take them with you?"

"We can, yes," Bohden replied.

"I don't want to leave my father," said Pearson with force and certainty as he stepped closer to the bed, away from Bohden.

"You need to, son; staying here is not an option."

Outside, Troy was worried things were not moving fast enough. He stepped over to speak with the pilots. "Talk to me. How close are they?" he asked through the open window.

The pilots looked at the radar screen, whereupon numerous neon signatures encroached with alarming speed. "Imperials will be within intercept range in less than eight minutes. You need to get these people onboard, Sergeant."

Troy nodded and told them, "Understood."

Hearing the pilot's warning, Troy rushed to meet Gale and Lambert, who were crossing the field to board. Troy stopped to urge them, "We're out of time. Whatever the holdup is, get it solved."

Lambert gave a stoic and understanding nod. "Lucy, go with Gale," he said as he turned to run back, stopping just outside the porch frame to yell, "Arlo!"

Arlo turned to see Lambert holding up his hand with all five fingers out. Arlo leaned across the door frame and shouted, "Bohden, it's time, let's go!"

"Alright, kids, you're with me, let's go," Bohden said as he rushed to gather everyone. Resisting him, however, was Eliza, who protested to stay. She tore her hand from Bohden's and then fell back toward her father, who she clung to desperately.

"Eliza, we have to go, please," Pearson said as he tried to pull his sister away.

"Listen to your brother, Eliza," pleaded Jeremiah as he held back a rush of tears.

At her father's order, Eliza finally released her grip and slipped back off the bed. Pearson took her by the hand and walked toward the door.

Just before watching his children leave for the last time, Jeremiah told them, "I love you both. Stay strong and listen to these men."

"We will," promised Pearson before taking Eliza from the room.

Jeremiah waited until he was alone with Bohden to ask him, "Please, watch over them."

"I will. You have my word."

With the Imperials only minutes away, the pilots throttled more power to the engine, causing the rotors to rise in speed and thrust to allow for the fastest exit. Once maximum idle was reached, the pilots again stressed the urgent need for take-off. "Sergeant! We are out of time!" one of the pilots said.

Crossing almost half of the field, Arlo stopped and faced the house. Just as he did, Pearson and Eliza rushed out the front door and dashed down the porch stairs. Arlo waved at them to run faster, but upon seeing Eliza struggling to keep up with Pearson, Arlo sprinted back to pick her up and carry her across the way.

Troy stood just outside of the whirling blades, ready and waiting to help everyone onboard. As Arlo arrived, Troy grabbed Eliza and lifted her in. After he strapped her into the grime-covered canvas seat, he noticed that her eyes were unresponsive and blank. Any presence of her had retreated, leaving nothing but a nervous system keeping her alive.

Once Eliza was secure, Gale leaned over to grab Pearson's hand to pull him inside. With both children onboard, the rest of the team jumped in and secured themselves for takeoff. The pilots then called out to Troy, "Is that everyone?"

"No! There's one more!" yelled Arlo in response.

"Where is he!?" Troy demanded as he stepped into the cabin. The front door then slammed behind Bohden as he emerged from the house. The six-foot-three giant pushed himself into the fastest sprint he could gather from what little strength he had left.

Crossing the distance, he came stumbling forward and leaped aboard like a runner over the finish line.

As the rugged aircraft lifted and took flight, a small cloud of dust and grass whirled in a spiral-like plume. Turning to the north, the pilots pulled the helicopter up and into a flight path out of the area. A loud rumble sounded all throughout the property as the aircraft passed the house and then disappeared across the fields.

CHAPTER 8

No more than five minutes after the team's exit, a flight of three Imperial helicopters descended upon the farmstead. After briefly circling the property, all three aircraft landed in formation upon the grass fields.

Trailing just behind the fleet was a convoy of ominous black vehicles approaching the property via the dirt road. When they arrived, the vehicles stopped just short of the house. There were five trucks in total, each the same as the other, square flat black frames outfitted with obsidian windows.

Sheridan emerged from the middle vehicle, followed closely by a small squadron of Imperial soldiers, who marched toward the house.

Stepping across the gravel driveway, Sheridan stopped to assess the pillar of smoke still churning from the downed Imperial chopper. He briefly wondered how Arlo's team had managed such a thing.

Before ordering his squadrons to conduct their search, Sheridan heard the familiar sound of Harper's aircraft shaking the sky. He turned to face the distinct low rumble of the jet turbines, and there he saw Harper's eccentric vessel descending from the sky in a perfect vertical downward vector. Sheridan's stomach churned from trepidation, but he dared not show any fear or concern while in the presence of his men.

The aircraft landed, and the ramp at the back of the vehicle opened, lowering to allow the dreadful officer to emerge. This time, Harper was accompanied by a squadron of her own, but not one of a human nature. Walking in lockstep with her were eight humanoid machines, mechanized skeleton-like figures armed with rifles. Where there should have been flesh and muscle, instead there were sleek hydraulics and polished gears that cranked and pushed. Instead of heads with eyes, there were box-like shapes with lenses and sensors.

As Harper and her mechanized squadron arrived, Sheridan shouted to his men, "Officer on deck!"

Upon hearing the order, every member of Sheridan's unit stopped in their tracks and turned to face Harper.

"I would prefer to keep this brief. Colonel Broderick Sheridan, by order of the King, you are under arrest for failure to perform your duty as a royal officer."

"Why don't we skip the bullshit. You're not here on any order of the King," Sheridan replied, then raised his voice, shouting to his men. "Take a good look and see the future of the Empire! I warned you all about where things were headed, didn't I? While you all faithfully served, the politicians sold you out in the crooked halls of Parliament. They conspired to replace you, and now here is the proof of their efforts. Quite sooner than I expected. She claims that I've failed as an officer, but rest assured, those who pull her strings have failed you as leaders. Trust me when I say that if you don't join me now in refusing to accept this betrayal, it will be too late."

"Join him, and you all will die as traitors," replied Harper.

"We will not bow to machines," boasted Sheridan as he took the opportunity to draw his pistol from the holster on his hip. His men joined him in the mutiny, attempting to open fire upon Harper and her team. The effort, however, was futile as Harper's soldiers reacted with machine-driven reflexes. Within fractions of a second, eight precise rounds were fired, killing every human present.

Harper's hollow, machine-like eyes scanned and studied the lifeless corpses as they struck the ground. Her face remained cold and unaffected.

.   .   .

It had been only an hour since Arlo and his team escaped from the farm. Their retreat was preserved by avoiding Imperial radar via maintaining low altitude. In doing so, the pilots kept the aircraft no more than thirty feet above the woodland canopy. It was a clever but unnerving tactic, as there was little room for error or correction should something go wrong. As little as a startled flock of birds could mean a violent crash into the dense forest.

For the passengers in the back, it was a different story. There was an ethereal quality to flight that Arlo and his team knew well. Being above the earth gave an opportunity to reflect upon its affairs from above. It was a unique form of separation that had the ability to shift perspectives and viewpoints. It was a rare moment to be outside looking in.

Chance gave Arlo a seat with the best view, his chair hugging the edge of the open cabin. This allowed the wind and sky to envelop him with a refreshing stream of natural air. For him, it carried away the incessant smells of death and chaos that were ever so hard to expel from the sensory entanglement of trauma. His seat also allowed him a wide view of the verdant forest horizon. To Arlo, the dichotomy and contrast of the earth with its natural majesty made little sense as to why something so beautiful would ever play host to the violent and ferocious affairs of men.

Before he could dwell in his mind any longer, a loud, piercing warning alarm sounded from the cockpit instrument panel.

"Imperial rotor wings just entered the area," said one pilot.

"How many?" asked Troy.

"Looks like a flight of three to our one o'clock, and another to our six."

"Can they acquire us?"

"On radar, no, but they could get a visual if we continue on this path. Advise we shift course and hope they pass."

"Alright, do it."

The pilots made an aggressive course correction to avoid the Imperial scouting party about to cross their visual field. As the aircraft tilted and then banked, everyone's stomachs nearly come out of their mouths. In the same movement, the rapid shift in gravity caused them to feel as if they weighed a thousand pounds. The maneuver complete, the helicopter leveled back to an even flight above the forest some distance from its prior position.

The relief, however, didn't last long, as another alarm sounded from the cockpit. Again, the radar acquired more incoming hostile forces.

"Traffic. Traffic. Nine o'clock," blared the machine voice of the onboard computer.

"Hang on," shouted the pilot as he pulled the cyclic to the left. This time he banked the helicopter dangerously downward and into an opening in the forest that hosted a wide river. The jagged banks of the flowing stream were just enough to fit the full body of the aircraft and its rotor disc.

Once the chopper settled to a hover, Arlo looked down to see that the landing skids were only five feet from the water. At this shallow distance, the furious rotor winds battered the surface of the river, causing a thick haze of vapor to rise like steam from boiling water.

The situation stable for the moment, Bohden scrolled through the mapping on Gideon's watch. With his finger, he traced the river to find the nearest point on the path Gideon had laid out. He then told Troy, "There's a town at the end of the river that we can use; it's marked as abandoned."

The lead pilot offered his thoughts on the proposal. "That could work. I can drop you all off and lead the Imperials away. But I can't keep dodging 'em like this; we're too heavy in the back."

"How long will that take?" Troy inquired.

"Best thing would be to alert Echo group, have them come get you, but I want to make sure we get these guys away from your position."

"Alright, put us in," ordered Troy as he leaned back into the cabin.

·   ·   ·

After the brief but tense flight up the river, the helicopter emerged above the tree line. As the ragged vessel ascended above the pine canopy, the pilots were careful to keep the flight low, not exceeding the threshold of the radar ceiling.

The town itself as viewed through the cloudy cockpit window was a small collection of worn brick storefronts and country shops lining a derelict main road.

As the pilots leveled for landing, they passed a row of deserted rural storefronts. The helicopter's incessant winds shook the cracked and eroded ground, which had not been disturbed in years. Rocks and debris were stirred up by the rotor's cyclone and blasted every which way. Glass was shattered, and signs and letters knocked loose from stasis.

When the landing skids made contact with the crumbling asphalt, Troy was the first to leap out and secure the perimeter. He briefly scanned the desolate area with his rifle. Nothing. Just overgrown weeds and remnants of what was once a quaint country town.

The landing sight clear, Troy waved for everyone else to leap out.

Once the helicopter was empty, Troy approached the cockpit to speak with the pilots.

"I'll alert Echo group now," the lead pilot said. "Give us an hour to lead the Imperials away. Then Echo should be here to get you."

Troy gave a thumbs-up in response and then moved to a safe distance to allow for takeoff. With a subtle turn on the collective, the pilot gave the aircraft enough power for a vertical lift off, up and out of the town. He was careful to avoid the collapsing street signs that swayed back and forth.

Once the chopper was gone, Troy led the group toward what was once a thriving general store at the center of the town.

As Arlo followed, he looked across the street to where there was a two-story brick building with windows overlooking the main road that ran through the town. "Gale, can I get you in that building on overwatch?" asked Arlo.

"Sure thing," replied Gale as he broke from the group to take up his position.

"I'll keep you company," Lambert added, snapping his fingers for Lucy to follow.

With the butt of his rifle, Troy smashed out the glass of the general store's door. He reached his hand through and unlocked the eroded deadbolt. Upon entering, Troy panned his rifle across the store, taking in the weeds and roots that had grown up through the tile and were gripping the walls and shelves.

"What the hell happened to this place?" Arlo asked, his eyes scanning the bereft aisles.

"These towns depended on the local farmers and craftsmen, but decades of new regulations killed the supply lines. Once the shelves emptied, everyone packed up and moved to the city," Ezra said as he walked around to the grime-coated front counter.

Across the street, Gale and Lambert broke into the building by shouldering their way through a collapsing wooden door that led to a second-story office—one that overlooked the entire block of the town.

Lucy was first through to scout ahead. She rushed inside and attuned her senses in search of anything she could find. Lambert followed closely with his rifle at the ready. "Talk to me, Lucy. Anything?" asked Lambert. He received only a quiet whimper as the search turned up nothing.

The room clear, Gale looked around to find anything useful. Against the main wall were several dust-covered chairs beside an old oak desk, at one time used for accounting and records for the storefront below. Gale cleared the papers; he and Lambert then pushed the desk close to the window. The aging wooden frame creaked and howled as it moved across the corroded floor.

Once the desk was beside the window frame, Gale folded out the bipod stands on his rifle and rested the pegs on the desk. After several quick adjustments of his scope, Gale's crosshairs followed the main road in and out of town. Despite there being nothing hostile in view, Gale couldn't help but notice a sound approaching in the distance. As it came closer, his first thought was tank tracks. "You hear that?" he asked softly. Confused, Lambert replied, "Hear what?"

Gale picked up his rifle and moved to check the other set of windows that overlooked a large courthouse building that made up the northern end of town. As soon as Gale came to the grime-coated window, he noticed a green Imperial armored personnel carrier entering the town's perimeter. Following closely behind on foot was a squadron of five soldiers. "Contact. Imperial Armor, with a squad of five Legion," said Gale, gazing through the scope.

Determined to warn the others, Lambert rushed back to the window that overlooked the general store. He placed two fingers in his mouth and let out a whistle that sounded like a bird call. The sound was familiar to Arlo and Bohden, who ran to the front set of windows. Knowing Lambert's call meant an incoming threat, Arlo was careful not to expose himself. He leaned out just enough to see Lambert in the window.

Both soldiers locked eyes, then Lambert gave Arlo a series of hand signals. One was the shape of the letter "A" and the other was a following motion. The final was the number five. Arlo immediately ran back to Troy. With a nervous tension, he said, "Imperial Armor with a scouting party."

"Did they acquire us?" asked Troy.

"Not yet, no. But we gotta hide," said Arlo as he looked for options.

"We can try upstairs, come on," said Troy.

Bursting through the rotten stairwell, Troy rushed to kick open the first door he found. Behind it was the main bedroom where the store's owner once lived.

Rushing inside, Arlo ran to the window where he could see that the Imperial forces had come to a stop in the middle of the road. Judging their movements, he realized it would be only seconds before they started searching buildings.

Bohden decided to work with what he had available. He checked the gap under the bed to see if Pearson and Eliza could fit. *It was neither the best choice nor the least obvious, but it could work,* he thought. Bohden quickly guided Pearson and Eliza to hide beneath the bed frame. He then turned his focus to Arlo and whispered, "Ezra and I will stay in here with them."

Arlo nodded and said, "We'll try the other room; if they find you, we'll close in."

Arlo and Troy searched for the next best option. They noticed there were two other doors, but if they were locked, it was too late to risk the sound of breaking them open. Arlo scanned the ceiling and saw a hatch that led to an attic. He gave a nod, prompting Troy to pull the hatch lever.

Attached to the attic door was a ladder that Troy folded out and climbed. Once secure, he turned and offered his hand to Arlo and, as he did, he heard glass shatter downstairs.

The Imperials were in the building.

Arlo was now more cautious as he scaled the ladder, careful to not make a noise that would draw attention. Once he was far enough, Troy pulled him up and closed the hatch behind them.

From the cobweb-infested attic, Arlo and Troy could hear one of the soldiers making his way up the stairs. They heard his heavy feet even from behind the walls. Each step produced a deep echo through the hollow, rotten building frame.

As the footsteps came closer, Pearson slid back farther away from the door. He held his hand tight over his sister's mouth, praying and hoping she wouldn't scream or cry. Just before the soldier pulled open the broken door, Pearson gave his sister a soft kiss on her head.

The door swung open, and Pearson saw a pair of black boots walk in and take several steps forward. The soldier then came to a stop. Pearson felt his sister's tears run down his hand.

In the closet beside the bed, Bohden and Ezra were hidden behind a row of old jackets and dresses. Through a small crack in the door, Bohden observed the soldier, and gauged his moves.

Before the Imperial continued his search, a transmission came in over his radio. "Two-one, report?"

The Imperial replied, "Two-one, all clear."

"Regroup on Hammer. We're moving out."

The transmission ended. The soldier turned and walked out of the room. But as soon as he did, he stopped for a moment. Another adrenaline rush came over Bohden as he watched the Imperial become suspicious of the fractured door. The soldier turned and scanned the room once more. His movements suggested he was going for the bed.

Bohden silently readied his pistol as he placed his free hand to open the closet door. As the soldier pressed into the mattress and leaned forward, Pearson knew he was about to be discovered. He gripped his sister tighter until . . . "Conor!" shouted a voice from downstairs. "They got 'em on radar, let's go!"

The urgency of the order was enough to pull the soldier away. As he rushed from the room, Pearson closed his eyes and softly let out a deep breath of relief through his nose. Finally, he was able to rest his hands and holster his pistol.

Outside, the sound of diesel and tank tracks

grinding forward was enough to allow Bohden and Ezra to emerge from hiding. Both men quietly stepped out. Bohden checked on Pearson and Eliza. He laid himself down to the ground where he could make eye contact, whispering, "I'm gonna make sure it's clear. Stay here."

Pearson simply nodded. His senses and nerves were too exhausted for anything else.

By the time Bohden emerged into the hallway, Arlo and Troy had come down from the attic.

"Close call?" wondered Arlo as Troy leaned to check the staircase.

"You don't want to know. . . . What were they doing here, anyway?" asked Bohden.

"Infinite resources. They'll search every inch of this forest if they have to."

Arlo asked, "How much farther to the border?"

"Not close enough to risk it on foot. They'll be back for us, just give 'em a chance," replied Troy.

.　　　.　　　.

Hour after hour passed, but there was no sign of the Americans returning for the rescue. The long wait gave

Gale and Arlo the chance to find the roof access of a building, one that allowed them a clear view of the horizon. Both men spent the final hours of daylight searching the empty skies for the hope of their extraction.

"Sun will be gone in 20 minutes; we should get a plan together for the night. Looks like we're staying here," said Arlo with a despondent gaze out to the skyline.

"Not sure if that's the best idea. The battery on that scrambler might not last the night. Imperials could have this area surrounded as soon as they acquire our signal."

"Well, we can't leave this position in case they return. Have you slept since we left Hutchinson?"

"No. Gave up on trying, honestly."

"You going to stay up here, then?"

"Yeah, I'll stay on watch. You and the others should get some sleep. I'll wake you if I catch something."

"Need anything?"

"If a food plan comes together, I could use some."

"Right. I'll see what we can do."

· · ·

The sun set, then a half-moon rose to take its place. The celestial luminary painted the town in a seamless pale blue. As night set in, the air was consumed by an unbroken ambience of forest insects that chirped and chimed from every part of the surrounding wilderness. This was a welcome gift, as it was the only assurance that life still existed beyond the haunting mood of the forgotten town.

In the bedroom above the general store, Bohden found himself on the night shift with Gale across the street. To pass the time, Bohden had set up a chessboard he'd found in the office.

With a set of night vision goggles in hand, Bohden watched Gale on the rooftop keeping track of the moves on a piece of paper. Setting down his pen, Gale grabbed his rifle and aimed it at the street. He flashed the infrared laser with one long burst followed by two short ones. He paused, and then flashed four quick bursts followed by one long. Bohden then moved the white bishop on the chessboard to square D4.

Bohden realized Gale would take his knight on the next move. "Cheeky bastard," said Bohden softly to himself, and snickered.

"What's wrong?" asked a voice in response. Bohden turned to notice Pearson standing in the doorway.

"Oh, nothing, just getting my ass kicked . . . again. . . . Come on in if you like."

"How are you playing?" asked Pearson as he took a seat beside Bohden.

"Here," Bohden said, offering Pearson the night vision goggles.

"Whoa," Pearson responded, overwhelmed by the sensation of night vision.

"Look out the window," said Bohden as he raised his rifle and flashed his infrared laser on the buildings across the way. "See that?"

"Yeah."

"We signal our moves in coded messages, morse code. But no matter how many times we play, I always end up in this same situation. I don't know how he does it.

"Can I help?" offered Pearson, returning the goggles to Bohden.

"By all means," Bohden replied, with an inquisitive look.

Pearson studied the board for several moments until telling Bohden, "He'll have you in check in a couple moves. Move your rook to take his pawn."

"I like my rook; I don't want to lose him."

"But you'll open the path for your bishop to take his queen in the next move. He'll try to counter instead of putting you in check."

Bohden looked at his pieces. Pearson was right. A smile formed on Bohden's face as he lifted his rook and removed Gale's pawn from the board. Bohden then flashed the play over to Gale.

Gale wrote the move on his wrinkled napkin, which also had his crude illustration of the game. Once he realized what Bohden had done, his face became puzzled. It was as if he was challenged for the first time in all their long years of unbalanced rivalry.

"Well, that stumped him," said Bohden with a grin.

"How do you know?"

"Because he usually sends me his move before I even finish telling him mine. How'd you learn to play?"

"My dad . . . taught me," Pearson said as he subtly choked on his words.

Eager to get the boy's mind off the trauma, Bohden asked him, "How's your sister doing?"

"Sleeping . . . surprisingly."

"Everyone responds to shock differently."

"Why couldn't you save him? What went wrong?"

"Trust me, if I could have, I would have."

"I just keep thinking I'm supposed to wake up. If I could wake up, then I could walk out of my room and see them both in the kitchen, making breakfast."

"Your sister probably feels the same, so what would you tell her?"

"That they're not coming back."

"Soon she will look to you for support, and you'll need to be there for her when it happens."

Pearson nodded his head with as much understanding as he could.

Bohden then observed Gale's message and told Pearson, "Pawn to B3, you were right."

.   .   .

About a block from the general store, there was a humble

white chapel that rested on the corner of an intersection. In the years that had passed since the abandonment, most of the exterior was consumed by rogue weeds and decay, but nonetheless the structure still stood against the inevitability of entropy. It was here that Arlo tracked down Ezra, who had broken into the chapel through the main double doors that had been boarded shut.

As Arlo entered, the harsh moonlit setting showed Ezra seated in the front row. Arlo made his approach, but his steps caused the floorboards to creak and moan. The invasive sound was enough to cause Ezra to turn back and notice.

"Shouldn't you be asleep?" Ezra said.

"Shouldn't you be with the group? I thought we agreed not to break off from each other."

"Couldn't sleep. I didn't want to keep the others up."

Arlo took a seat across the aisle. His eyes wandered and studied the eroding chapel architecture. "Surprised this building survived the Correction."

"From what I gathered, they turned it into a town hall for meetings. I assume there's been no sign of a rescue?"

"No, nothing."

After waiting for Ezra to say something, Arlo eventually said to him, "It's lonely in here."

"Yes. Gives me room to think."

"Something on your mind?"

"There was never a crash that I survived. I wasn't shot down. I was stationed at that house, just me. They told me a contact was coming to pass off the evidence to. They didn't give me much, just that someone was coming. . . . I didn't know how long I was supposed to wait, or what else I was supposed to try. All I had was my loyalty and my trust. I guess that's why I never said anything. I couldn't afford to let you doubt the Americans while asking you to join them. Even though it was likely they had forgotten about me . . . and the mission they told me was so vital."

"So then what is truly waiting for us in the Neutral Zone?"

"The Americans use the humanitarian corridors there to smuggle everything from weapons to personnel. My plan is to get us passage to the American leadership and confront them about why they abandoned trying to prove the truth."

"Why tell me this now?"

"Because I want you to do it. I've seen what your leadership is capable of, and it's something the Americans need more than anything right now. Especially if there is truly to be a new nation at the end of all this."

"A new nation, huh?" said Arlo as he leaned back to think on Ezra's words.

"You don't believe me?"

"No, I think at this point, it might just be crazy enough to try."

Ezra stood and walked across the aisle to present Arlo with a hard drive he'd pulled from his jacket pocket.

"What's this?" asked Arlo.

"The evidence, all of it."

"Why are you giving it to me?"

"It's my way of knowing that you accept what I've proposed."

Arlo looked down to the drive in Ezra's hand, then slowly reached out to accept it. "You sure about this?"

"Very," Ezra replied as he stepped away and headed for the chapel door. It slammed shut behind him.

Arlo found himself in profound silence and emptiness. The derelict walls deadened the ambience of the outside world, leaving him with a deprivation of all sensory stimulus, finally offering him the chance for a moment's rest.

Closing his eyes, Arlo was immediately plunged into a lucid dream, the landscape of which was a golden wheat field that extended in all directions as rolling hills. The sky was filled with cosmic magnificence, the galactic band and the billion luminaries it hosted in full view, even in the broad light of day.

Just ahead, Arlo saw Gideon walking through the field slowly. Arlo ran to him, but the closer he came to Gideon, the more time itself was hindered to a slow crawl. Despite the phenomena, Arlo pressed forward as if wading through the mud of a dense swamp. As his body disturbed the wheat, he could see that it moved like molded clay.

When Arlo finally reached Gideon, he fought the drag of freezing time and managed to raise his arm to grab him by the shoulder. Just as his hand touched the metal plate of Gideon's armor, Gideon was blown away like ash in a gust of wind. The eerie, bizarre phantasm continued to cascade outward, morphing the entire landscape of the dream into dust.

To Arlo's astonishment, the dust was being drawn and carried by the wind toward a fixed point in the sky. When it all had coalesced, there was nothing but an empty black all around. Strangely, however, Arlo could see a glistening object falling from the sky where the current had taken the dismantled world.

With a sudden desperate urge, he sprinted to catch the object before it crashed to the ground. Time no longer hindered, he was able to reach it.

It fell into his hands.

He realized it was an hourglass filled with sand.

CHAPTER 9

It was morning and everyone awoke to the disappointment of no American rescue.

As the first rays of sunrise touched the destitute town, Arlo stood in the middle of the intersection. With a hopeless gaze he stared down the street until Lambert emerged from the general store. Joining Arlo, he told him, "Gale and Bohden checked the other buildings. No sign of him."

"I don't get it. Why did he run?"

"If the other American had gone with him, I'd be more worried, but sounds like this is something he did on his own. Did he say anything to you at all?"

"No. Just gave me the evidence and said that it belonged with me."

"Well, 'least he gave you what we need."

"Hopefully."

"I also hate to bring more bad news, but the

scrambler has only got about an hour of battery life."

"I know."

"I looked over the map again. The border is only thirty miles or so from here. At this point, they're gonna spot us, anyways. I say we salvage one of these cars and just make a dash for it."

"I was thinking the same thing."

"Great minds, right?"

"I'm not so sure anymore. I'm beginning to think that you've been right all along. If I had just gone with you all to the bar, I wonder where we would be now."

Lambert placed his hand on Arlo's shoulder. "Who cares? I'd do it all over if it meant learning the truth. Can't put a price on that."

"Good to know," said Arlo, shrugging off his doubts.

.   .   .

Having spent his late youth boosting cars for fast money, Bohden was the most qualified for the task of reviving one of the many abandoned vehicles within the town.

In a parking lot behind the main street, Bohden

and Pearson found an old, rusted pickup truck that at one point in its life was painted a seamless sky blue. Easily the most dated vehicle left behind, Bohden chose it for its simplicity and potential for repair. Anything else was too new and would most likely require repairs to the onboard computer systems, something he had no knowledge of.

Making his assessment on the engine of the old truck, he determined that all the vehicle needed was a new battery. The plugs were still good, and there was enough oil left for the truck to make one more voyage. Bohden's search for a battery led him and Pearson to break into the other abandoned cars that filled the lot. By the end of their search, they had gathered and tried seven dust-covered batteries in total.

"Alright, crank it!" shouted Bohden from beneath the hood of the car after connecting the final battery.

"Okay!" said Pearson from behind the wheel of the truck.

After receiving a crash course in keyless ignition from Bohden, Pearson grabbed and crossed the starter wires from beneath the dash. As he finessed the connection, Bohden listened to the engine cough and struggle to turn over. Several long cycles of rising and falling, as well as teasing Bohden with the hope of engaging, the motor eventually gave in and turned over. A sudden loud bang sounded, and then a plume of thick black smoke came out of the exhaust pipe.

"Give it some gas! Hurry!" urged Bohden.

Pearson pressed his foot onto the peddle. Once the engine was stable and running, a small smile formed on Bohden's face. "Alright! We got it!"

"It's working!?" Pearson asked in disbelief.

"Can't you tell?"

"Barely!"

"Right, well hop out. We need to get some gas for this thing."

"Where are we gonna get gas?"

"I'll show you."

Bohden grabbed both a long black hose and a red gas container he had found amidst the leftovers of the town. They then wandered the parking lot, looking for a vehicle with an accessible fuel door. The easiest target was a corroded station wagon Pearson found behind one of the crumbling brick buildings.

As Bohden came around to the fuel door, he wedged a screwdriver into the hatch and forced it open.

Fuel cap exposed, he pulled it off and shoved the hose into the tank.

"What are you doing?" asked Pearson, raising his brow in curiosity.

"It's called a siphon. This is how I used to get gas before the service."

"You stole it?" Pearson said.

"Life was different back then. *I* was different," replied Bohden as he cut the hose with his knife to create a smaller tube for the siphon. "Here. Stand back," Bohden ordered as he put the hose in his mouth and sucked the fuel forward.

"Oh shit!" said Pearson, stepping back in concern.

Bohden felt the gas reach the tip. He pulled out the hose, but not fast enough to avoid spilling a full serving into his mouth. Bohden tried to gag, cough, and spit, but it wasn't much help. He noticed Pearson could not help but laugh as Bohden struggled to recover. "Yeah, yeah, joke's on me," he declared as he guided the hose into the gas can.

As it slowly filled, Bohden thought to himself that it might be worth it to do all over again if it meant giving Pearson another smile, another moment to take his focus off the fallout.

Then Bohden's eyes went wide as he heard the familiar sound of an incoming missile echoing throughout the sky. He instinctively traced the sound of the jet-driven whistle to see the rocket burst through the immediate layer of clouds and turn downward for a strike on the town. "Run!" shouted Bohden as he grabbed Pearson.

Before making it to any semblance of safety, the missile struck near the main road, some distance from Bohden's position. The seismic force of the explosion rippled across the town. Bohden turned back to see a massive storm of debris and smoke swirling and expanding upward from the aftermath of the strike. "Wait here," he said with an authoritative urgency as he rushed back to the town and into the destruction.

Bohden raced through a nearby brick alley that was flooding with a cloud of yellow smoke. As it enveloped him in a ghostly embrace, he pulled his tattered shirt up above his mouth to filter the toxic air. When he emerged onto the main street, he quickly discerned that the missile had struck a distant building some hundred yards from the location of Arlo and the others.

Puzzled and confused, Bohden looked the other way to see Arlo and the rest of the team out in the street, as well. "You alright!?" shouted Bohden as he ran to join Arlo.

An Imperial aircraft, Harper's, abruptly emerged through the smoke column of the air strike and made a rapid vertical descent onto the jagged asphalt. Once the jet thrust leveled the vehicle for a solid touchdown, the engines switched to idle.

A voice shouted through a loudspeaker: "You are surrounded. Lower your weapons and surrender. This is your only warning."

Arlo quickly debated his options, but they were few. He knew the missile was a warning shot, a display of force should he and his men fail to comply. Outgunned by the ambush of the Empire, Arlo gave his men a subtle nod, telling them to comply.

One after the other, each soldier tossed down their rifles. Lambert however, concealed a loaded pistol in the waistband of his pants. "Lambert. . . ." Arlo cautioned, advising him to reconsider.

"I don't intend to go quietly."

"Just be patient. They want us alive or that missile would have struck our position directly. We still have a chance here."

The cargo ramp at the back of the aircraft lowered to reveal Harper as she stepped out. Escorting her was her drone squadron, which was something Arlo and his men had not yet witnessed. Upon seeing their other worldly opponent, Arlo's team did everything to keep themselves from being drawn into surreal disassociation.

"What the hell is going on?" asked Lambert to the group.

"Our intelligence mentioned that the Empire was experimenting with non-human combatants . . . but they said they were just in preliminary trials," answered Troy in disbelief.

"Doesn't look very preliminary, mate," Bohden replied.

"Alright, everyone form up," commanded Arlo of his team, to which Troy responded, "Form up!? For what?"

"We're in this to form a new nation, are we not? It's time we started acting like one." Arlo then stepped forward to meet Harper's approach. One by one, each man joined the formation, Lambert being the last and the most cautious. Once everyone was in place, Arlo stood in the middle with Gale on his right, Bohden to his left. Lambert stood at the end to finish the line with Troy.

"The hell are you doing!?" scolded Arlo at the sight of Pearson, who was running to join their formation.

"I'm willing to fight . . . sir!"

"No, get back inside. Now," replied Arlo.

"Can you shoot?" Lambert asked.

Pearson nodded.

"Good enough for me. We need all the help we can get. Let him stand with us, Arlo."

"It's fine if he can shoot, but I'm not sure what guns are gonna do at this point," added Gale as he eyed the whining pistons and gears of the drone units.

"I'll keep 'im with me, Arlo," Bohden said before Arlo could reject the idea.

Harper and her squadron came to a stop no more than fifteen feet from Arlo. The eyes of both leaders locked in silent fury. Harper's gaze then moved across Arlo's line to gain an assessment of her opposition. She said to them all, "I came to offer terms. If you comply and come peacefully, I have been given the King's word that your punishment will be merciful."

"We are the independent and sovereign nation of America," replied Arlo. "We recognize no King, nor his handlers. We will entertain neither demands nor threats."

Unmoved and unconvinced, Harper's machine eyes glared back for some time until she finally told him, "Allow me to assure you that the second strike will not be a warning."

"You came to offer terms, so here are ours: Go back to London, leave us to establish prosperity in peace, or suffer the consequences," Arlo replied.

"Consequences? Is this your attempt at humor?"

"Unless for some odd reason, Parliament has suspended the Combat Accords, then articles 45 and 46 are still in effect, are they not? In which case, you and the rest of the Empire are obligated to grant all foreign powers under Imperial siege a twenty-four-hour grace period to either evacuate non-combatants or peacefully surrender before the application of lethal force."

"The Combat Accords are over a hundred years old, and this is not a siege."

"They may be old, but they were never recalled, and a siege is defined as any body or members of a foreign nation surrounded by military force—which you kindly informed us was the case when you rode in here."

"You are not a foreign power. You are traitors."

"Wrong. Article 12, paragraph 19 of the accords dictates that charges of treason do not apply to Imperial citizens once asylum has been granted by a foreign power, which in this case would be America. Therefore, we are no longer traitors, but if you need a label, then you may refer to us as foreign actors, which still falls within the parameters of Articles 45 and 46. Which, may I remind you, state that any member of the Imperial Army who willingly defies an article of the accords are themselves guilty of treason and shall hang from the rope. In your case, though, they may reconsider the manner of execution."

In response to Arlo's legal challenge, Harper's computer-driven mind went to work, calculating and cross-referencing the statements for their validity.

"Means fuck off. We'll speak to you tomorrow," said Lambert.

Harper seamlessly turned and led her squadron in another rhythmic march back to her aircraft.

Once the threat subsided, Bohden praised Arlo's

maneuver. "Clever move, chief."

"I can admit when I'm impressed, but not sure what this gets us," said Troy.

"Time," Arlo stressed.

Once inside her transport, Harper moved with a furious pace to her communications panel, a large computer system near the cockpit of the vehicle. She sent a transmission to a secretive source, one with no name or location. When the call was answered, the digital image of a censored, distorted human face displayed upon the video call screen.

The anonymous specter was first to speak. "Do you have them?"

"They have invoked the articles of the Combat Accords. They claim they are a new nation under siege."

"What!? That is absurd!"

"I cannot violate Imperial Law without a directive from the King. My programming inhibits it."

"Forget the King. You have our directive. Kill them."

"I would still need voice authorization."

"Then get into position for a strike on the town and open a channel for remote access to the weapon system. . . . It's not a violation if we pull the trigger."

"Consider it done," said Harper as she powered off the transmission and then rushed to the cockpit of the aircraft. Awaiting her command were two more humanoid droids programmed as pilots. "Get us airborne and then arm H5 missiles. Target every human signature in that town."

Each unit gave a subtle nod followed by powering up the turbine engines.

As Harper's aircraft lifted from the ground, the vehicle turned to face Arlo's team. Once a steady hover was achieved, two metal hatches along the wingspan retracted to display several missile batteries. Arlo's team took quick notice of the hostile gesture. "Looks like they may be reconsidering," said Lambert.

"Take cover. Now!" Arlo commanded as they all dashed in the futile hope of surviving the assault.

Just as both missiles ignited, scalding tracer rounds fired from an incoming fighter jet bombarded the street, tearing apart the would-be strike in the same motion. Following less than a second behind were two low-flying fighter jets of unknown origin. In one continuous procession, both jets soared across the town and fired two guided missiles that struck the right engine of Harper's aircraft. Without a second engine to hold the vehicle level, it began to spiral out of control, rising and falling in altitude, eventually drifting into the forest and crashing into the canopy with a colossal explosion.

Following directly behind the saving airstrike were two heavy helicopters. The deep thunder of the rotors was a welcome sound as it shook the town. Both choppers stacked in a column formation for a rapid landing in the street. As the aircraft settled upon the asphalt, Arlo could clearly see Gideon leaping out from the cabin and running toward him.

"I don't fuckin' believe it," said Lambert.

Gideon waved his hand urgently for Arlo's team to get onboard. Even with the torrent of noise from the rotor blades, Arlo could hear Gideon's voice shouting, "Let's go! Let's go!"

"What happened to you!?" urged Arlo as he met Gideon.

"I'll explain later. Let's get everyone on board. We gotta do this now!"

As Arlo's team sprinted to the helicopters, both fighters returned for a flyby of the town. The sonic boom of their passage left a piercing echo in the air as they crossed the sky within seconds. Over Gideon's radio came the pilot's voice saying, "Liberty, this is Falcon 3. Good effect on target. Visual on all friendlies. We're RTB to rearm and reengage. Over."

Once inside the rotor wash of the helicopters, Arlo directed Bohden, shouting, "You and Troy take the kids in the other chopper!"

At Arlo's order, Bohden nodded, guiding Pearson and Eliza to board the second aircraft.

In a far more familiar way, Pearson leaped aboard and turned to take his sister from Bohden. He then settled her into the canvas seat and secured her with the restraints. Pearson could see that Eliza had been pushed further into shock by the chaos. Her eyes were now dead and hollow.

Bohden and Troy leaped aboard and tethered themselves in the cabin.

After takeoff, both helicopters turned for a northbound departure, directly toward the border of the Neutral Zone. With the flight underway, Arlo approached Gideon in the aircraft and pressed him to answer. "Gideon, just what the hell is going on?"

"We decided it was time to intervene."

"We? Who's we!?"

"I represent another faction in this fight. We exist to prevent artificial intelligence from taking over human government. Which the Empire has initiated with their recent actions."

"You mean the drones?"

"Not just the drones. The entire leadership of the Empire is now under the complete direction of an artificial intelligence."

"Why did you wait until now to act!?"

"Our laws dictate that we cannot engage an enemy based on the assumption of a crime. We had to let them choose this."

"Then why did you intervene against Wallcroft?" Lambert asked, joining the discussion.

"I never said I was there for Wallcroft."

"Then why were you there?" demanded Arlo.

"I don't answer to you. But once again your lack of appreciation for rescue is noted."

"I'll speak for all us, then—thank you. But what now? What the hell are we supposed to do?" Lambert asked.

"The Empire has sent the world down a grim timeline. They will deploy their AI army against the Americans, claiming it necessary to deal with heightened threats. Eventually, they will abandon their identity as the British Empire, and they will reorganize under a centralized system managed and maintained by an artificial intelligence. Many will not accept it and the world will descend into war."

"How do you know all this?" Arlo inquired with deep suspicion.

"I'm not at liberty to discuss that: just know that Ezra's idea won't work anymore. Everything has changed."

"How do you know about him?"

"I can't answer that."

"Then what is something you will answer!?"

"The plan forward, which is to convene a congress of the American leadership. If we can win this, then America will need to exist. The republic they plan to create is the only means to restore this timeline."

"Timeline? What do you mean, timeline?" asked Arlo, who was interrupted by a blaring warning alarm sounding from the cockpit.

"Shit! Missile lock! Two of 'em!" warned the pilot.

"How!? We crossed the Neutral Zone!" said Gideon.

"Doesn't look like they care anymore," the pilot replied. "Deploying chaff!" shouted the co-pilot in response.

From a row of fixed canisters on both aircraft, numerous sparkling flares were fired out and surrounded the pair of helicopters. As the dazzling light from the chaff expanded and drifted into the wind, the approaching missiles redirected to the heat signature of the brilliant light.

"Brace yourselves!" ordered Gideon just before impact.

The first missile, intended for Bohden's craft struck the chaff and detonated at a distance. However the second missile struck much closer to Arlo's vessel, sending a scalding shockwave outward that consumed all oxygen in the area, causing Arlo's helicopter to suffer an engine failure.

With the power to the rotors cut, the pilot skillfully activated the auto-rotate, allowing the force of free-fall to spin the rotors. After a violent shake rippled through the cabin, control of the aircraft was restored, enough to allow the pilots to maneuver into a controlled crash landing.

"Hang on!" said the main pilot. All he could see ahead of him was unbroken forest.

From the open cabin of his helicopter, Bohden watched as the second aircraft fell into the forest with a ripping descent. He saw the rotors cut into the trees and break apart as the aircraft crashed beyond visibility. Overtaken by the sight, Bohden demanded to his pilots, "Bring us around and put me in!"

"There's nowhere to land!" countered the pilot.

"Then I'll use the rope! Put me in! Now!"

Following Bohden's order, the pilot abruptly leveled the helicopter to a hover, allowing Bohden to pull the retaining pin on the fast rope mounted to a pulley system outside of the cabin. Once the pin was pulled, the long black rope went loose and fell to the ground. Before jumping, Bohden turned to tell Troy, "Don't follow; just get them out of here."

As he jumped, Bohden swung out with the rope and then began his slide to the ground. The moment his boots touched the forest floor, the pilot pressed the cargo release, and then the latches jettisoned the rope.

CHAPTER 10

The concussive force of being thrown from the helicopter crash left Lambert momentarily unconscious. His tattered body lay motionless in the dirt as Lucy poked and clawed at him, whining and whimpering. Eventually, Lambert regained himself and was able to lift from the loose dirt. The impact left him bruised and slow, but his fortunes could have been far worse, as he realized he was only several feet from a row of trees.

Following a sluggish and disoriented rise, he turned to see the hazy image of Arlo running toward him.

"You alright!?" yelled Arlo as he arrived to help.

"I'll make it," grunted Lambert, who then stood on his own and said, "Get to the crash; I'll be right behind you."

Being torn apart from numerous collisions, the wreckage of the helicopter had finally settled cockpit-first against a towering pine. As best he was able, Gale worked to lift one of the dead pilots out from the shattered glass of the cockpit. His hope was that there was still a chance to resuscitate.

When Arlo arrived at the crash with tired lungs, he looked into the cabin to see that the second pilot suffered the same lethal fate. His body was crushed by the collapsed aircraft frame.

From the other side, Gideon emerged nearly unaffected, save for several scratches and dents in his armor. "Search party will be here soon; we need to keep moving," he said hurriedly.

"Move to where? This was supposed to be the safe zone," responded Lambert as he limped his way to join the group.

"I saw a clearing on the way down; we should try to make it there for extraction. I'll radio for backup," Gideon concluded.

Bohden's voice then called out from within the forest. "Arlo? Lambert?"

"Over here!" Arlo yelled back.

Bohden appeared from the distance and found the others waiting for him. His voice was exhausted and his breathing heavy. "Glad to see you're all in one piece."

"Did the other chopper make it out?" asked Arlo.

"From what I could tell."

"Enough chatting. Follow me," urged Gideon before leading the way back into the forest. He initiated a transmission over his radio. "Liberty, this is two-five. We lost our transport and are proceeding on foot to nearest extraction point. We have wounded and are being pursued by Imperial forces. Requesting immediate air support. Coordinates to follow."

In response, an authoritative voice came back over Gideon's radio. "Liberty copies all, two-five. Tasking gunship support to your area. ETA ten minutes."

"Where the hell did you get this kind of backup?" Bohden asked.

"He can't answer that question," replied Lambert with skepticism.

"What I don't reveal is for your own protection. I suggest you start believing me," Gideon said as he armed himself with a grenade launcher. He fired it at the wreckage of the helicopter. Upon detonation, the grenade released a cloud of molten thermite that began to melt and consume the frame of the helicopter. Gideon then added, "Can't risk the Imperials recovering our technology. Anything happens to me, I expect you to do the same."

.   .   .

Within a mile, Gideon guided Arlo's team to a sizeable forest clearing, a large meadow where there was also a meager farming village of archaic stone houses. Surrounding the humble buildings were countless rolling hills that hosted fields and crops, all of which were bordered by the seemingly infinite forest line.

As they came upon the perimeter of the clearing, everyone settled from their rush and hid themselves within the trees, obscuring their presence from any potential Imperials.

Taking a knee beside a wide pine, Gideon scanned the village with the computer-driven lenses fixed to his intricate mask. "I'm not seeing any movement down there. Might be best to hide in the village and wait out extraction," he offered.

"How long till your people can get to us?" Arlo asked.

"I don't know. This wasn't supposed to happen," Gideon replied as he grabbed his radio for a transmission.

Opening the channel, he said into the mic, "Liberty, this is two-five. We are entering a local village to await extraction."

Cautiously exiting the forest, Gideon led Arlo and his men through the waist-high brush of a wheat field and then into the vacant village filled with evidence of a sudden evacuation. Containers of seeds and grain were spilled over, tools were dropped in place from a desperate escape and, much to the team's concern, all of it appeared to have been recent.

As they moved farther, the passage corralled everyone down a single dirt path that ended at the center of the village. A herd of loose chickens and sheep startled the team as the panicked animals ran to safety in the field.

"Any idea what happened here?" Bohden asked as he looked over the empty setting.

"Looks like something spooked 'em," offered Gale.

"The sooner we get out of sight the better, no?" Lambert asked, as he moved to check one of the stone huts.

Before turning the corroded handle of the front door, Lambert gave a quiet order to Lucy, telling her to wait. He gave one more look back to his team, who had settled to a knee, waiting for him to confirm the house was empty.

Lambert gently pushed the old wooden door open, his eyes following the light as it fell upon the interior of the house, revealing a worn floor rug that hosted a small archaic kitchen table and chairs. Lucy followed him closely with a perceptive posture. She then began to sniff the air, causing her to give a subtle whine that warned them that they were not alone.

Lambert abruptly panned his rifle toward the back corner and flashed the area with the light affixed to his gun. Illuminated on the floor of the kitchen was a young woman and her child, a boy. As the light fell on them, she pulled her child in close and shielded him.

To calm the woman and her child, Lambert placed his finger against his lips, gesturing them to remain quiet. As he did this, his focus was exploited by another figure in the home, the father who leaped over the kitchen counter and charged Lambert with a knife.

With just enough time to prevent Lucy from mauling the father, Lambert grabbed her by the collar and held her back as he was tackled to the ground. "No! No!

No!" shouted Lambert as the knife was thrust into his right shoulder.

Before the frightened villager could follow through with a stab to Lambert's neck, Arlo arrived and tossed the villager off and away. In the struggle, Lucy finally broke free and, with snarling teeth and deep growls, she charged Lambert's attacker. "Lucy! No!" ordered Lambert, halting the attack.

To finally ease the chaos, Bohden raised his rifle and shouted, "Drop the fucking knife, you moron. We're friendly."

In response, the villager yelled back in a language foreign to all but Gideon. "He won't understand you; that's Gaelic he's speaking," stated Gideon.

"What the hell is that?" Bohden wondered.

"Old Irish. They live on these lands."

"Can you understand him?" asked Arlo.

"My system can translate it, but I don't know how well," Gideon replied.

"Well, tell him we're not here to hurt him. We thought the village was empty," Lambert said, recovering.

Gideon told the villager in his native tongue,

"We're not your enemy. We thought we could take shelter here. We're sorry."

The villager shouted back at Gideon, prompting Arlo to ask, "What is he saying?"

"I . . . I don't know. Something about a giant they're hiding from. Says it's a monster."

"What!?" Bohden exclaimed.

"He probably doesn't know what a helicopter is. He probably confused the sound," replied Arlo.

"How about we stop playing into this and get inside," Lambert said as he pressed a fresh gauze pad against the knife wound.

"I said it was a flying machine, not a monster, but he said something was dropped in by an aircraft, maybe multiple, I can't tell," said Gideon as he struggled to interpret the panicked voice.

Confused and frustrated, Lambert asked, "What the fuck does that mean?"

As the villager continued to clamor back, a single seismic pulse rocked the ground. It was as if a building had collapsed, or a bomb had been dropped. Following the quake-like pulse was another just like it, and then another. The rhythm was as if something was walking. In response to the phenomenon, the villager ran back inside his house, the terror familiar. As Arlo and his team desperately tried to trace the source of the booming ground thunder, the origin was finally revealed.

Just outside the village, a wall of trees was broken apart by a towering testament of Imperial force. When the dust settled, a ten-meter-tall humanoid machine became visible. The goliathan robot was built with four limbs: two arms, two legs, and a central torso that hosted a cockpit. Each arm of the predatory mech unit was equipped with massive artillery canons, Gatling guns, and gauss rifle-like launchers. Atop the shoulder brackets and pistons were rectangular missile systems capable of long-range efficacy.

"Fuck all," muttered Gideon as he took in the spectacle.

Within a moment of its arrival, the mech, known by its Imperial designation, Man-O-War, acquired Arlo and his team via thermal scan from its sensor array. Once a positive lock was confirmed by the targeting computer, a barrage of devastation was unleashed upon the village. Two missiles were fired from the shoulder launchers, followed by two artillery shells from the arm canons. All this obscured the Man-O-War in a thick veil of exhaust smoke and spent propellant.

The artillery, which was fired in a horizontal path, was first to strike the village, detonating upon impact with the stone surface of the houses. The explosion created a two-story kinetic cloud of dirt and stone that fell in a heavy rain of debris. The strike disturbed the remaining villagers in hiding. They fled from their dwellings like a frenzied herd, desperately trying to escape into the wheat fields with their children and livestock.

The missiles, fired in an arch-like pattern, were next to hit. Anti-personnel by nature, the missiles produced a smaller, more focused destruction that demolished the house Arlo and Gideon were hiding behind. The force of the detonation blew both men some ten feet through the air.

Gideon, who landed in a small crop, was first to recover; he climbed out of the broken plants and dashed to rescue Arlo, who he found buried under the wreckage of a collapsed chicken coop. As he gripped Arlo's arm, he yanked him out and pulled him to cover behind another rock wall. "You alright!?" asked Gideon.

Arlo simply replied with a dust-covered thumbs up.

At the other end of the village, Lambert guided Gale and Bohden to cover behind a collapsed stone house.

"Why is it that on the one fucking day that we decide to go to war with the Empire, they unleash this shit on us!? Is it really this bloody personal?" shouted Lambert who was answered by another round of artillery fired from the Man-O-War. This time, the shells whistled past the village and struck the forest, blasting timber over twenty yards into the air.

Gideon called again for help over the radio. "Liberty, this is two-five. We have engaged enemy armor at the extraction site. We need air support now!"

In a monotone, detached reply, Gideon was told, "Understood, two-five, but be advised all our air assets are currently engaging Imperial forces in the area. Advise you hold your position until they can get to you."

"And I advise that you get eyes on this fucking thing! There wasn't supposed to be a Man-O-War here!"

"Copy that, two-five. We will survey the area and keep you updated."

"Doesn't sound like they're interested," said Arlo as the transmission ended.

"They'll come, but we need to buy some time. Take these and toss 'em to the north," said Gideon, who gave Arlo two large smoke grenade canisters.

Gideon abruptly took off running to the other side of the village. When he was halfway across, he pulled the pin on a smoke grenade and tossed it toward the Man-O-War, which was adjusting for another barrage. On the opposite side of the village, Arlo did the same, tossing both of his smoke grenades into the northern field.

Tumbling through the grass, all four canisters ignited with a sudden spark and then began billowing out small plumes of rapidly expanding white smoke. Within several moments, the entire field was enveloped, obscuring the Man-O-War's thermal sensors.

Upon realizing he could no longer lock onto Arlo's team via the main computer, the pilot at the helm of the Man-O-War toggled several switches on his elaborate console. Loud levers from deep within the cabin echoed as the main canons reengaged. With a subtle trigger pull on the joysticks, he fired all four canons blindly into the smoke.

The first two shots passed over the village and fell into the fields behind, killing nearly all the villagers in retreat. The next two shots impacted within the village, detonating close enough to Lambert that he and Bohden were abruptly consumed by a cascade of exploded dirt and smoke.

Recovering from the shockwave, Bohden quickly realized Gale was missing. Frantically, he crawled back to the blast zone where he could hear Gale's screams for help beneath a heap of jagged rocks. In desperation, Bohden heaved the debris off the pile and found Gale beneath. As he lifted him out, Bohden could see Gale's femur was crushed and limp.

As the Man-O-War reloaded its canons for another barrage, Gideon knew he had to improvise if the team was to survive. He quickly glanced toward the field, and then over to Arlo who was sheltering across the small road. Confident he could make it, he leaped out from cover and sprinted to Arlo.

Sliding across the dirt and into the stone wall Arlo was ducking behind, Gideon didn't waste a second before telling him, "Take my radio. It's set to the frequency of my army. Get back into the forest and survive until air support arrives."

"What!?" shouted Arlo, who was then interrupted by another assault of artillery that went whistling over the village.

"Just do it, Arlo! Now!" screamed Gideon as he shoved Arlo out from cover and toward his team. Gideon then typed commands into his wrist computer to initiate a cloak that encased him in distorting reality until vanishing completely.

From his view through the Man-O-War's cockpit, the pilot could see the village through the fading smoke. With nothing left to obscure the thermal image, the pilot watched as the computer targeting locked onto four signatures hiding in the area, all of which were Arlo's team.

Just as the pilot gripped the trigger, Gideon reappeared near the left leg of the Imperial behemoth. Gideon aimed his grenade launcher precisely at the unit's intricate knee joint. Aligning his sights, Gideon fired a propelled grenade from his launcher. As the explosive collided with its target, a cloud of scalding thermite was released, which instantly began to melt and warp the knee joint of the Man-O-War's left leg. With each passing second of the thermite's reaction with the metal, the Man-O-War became more unstable. Eventually, the towering mechanical giant collapsed onto its afflicted knee, rocking the ground with seismic force.

Gideon sprinted forward to climb the colossal machine. As he did, the pilot finally acquired Gideon and opened fire with the Gatling gun affixed to the Man-O-War's opposite arm. Hoping to prevent the impending sabotage, the pilot chased Gideon with a barrage of gunfire, but it was too close of a target. Gideon had just barely escaped the pilot's field of view and was able to grab a hold of the Man-O-War's embossed armor plating. With courage and force, Gideon scaled the height of the machine, leaping from one gripping point to another.

To thwart Gideon's ascent, the pilot turned and moved the Man-O-War with jerking motions, hoping to toss Gideon like a bothersome insect. Even as his fingers slipped and struggled, Gideon's strength held on long enough for him to reach the access hatch of the cockpit. From there, Gideon was able to hold a firm grip around the main handle while he fired grenade after grenade into every vital wire and structure. After shooting a fifth round, both of the Man-O-War's arms melted through their joint fixtures and were beginning to break away from the torso, like ripping flesh.

With only one round remaining, Gideon aimed his launcher directly—and dangerously—downward at the roof of the cockpit. Just as he fired his last shot, he was finally thrown from the Man-O-War by a momentous turn of the torso.

Falling almost two stories, Gideon collided with the dirt of the grass field, tumbling and rolling some distance before having the chance to look back and see an inevitable molten deluge expanding to consume what little remained of the Man-O-War.

Gideon's victory was short-lived as he heard the rising whine of power being transferred to the right arm canon that had not yet fallen off.

Gideon leaped up and sprinted as fast as he was able, but the open field that he fell into made him an easy target.

As the Man-O-War tracked Gideon, he frantically typed a command into his wrist computer. Inputting the order, a digitized voice spoke to him from within the display of his mask, telling him, "Warning! Phase Shift Drive has not cleared experimental use and is not authorized without override command."

"Override authorization two-five-Alpha!" shouted Gideon as he came to a stop and stared down the artillery barrel of the Man-O-War.

"Please note that phase shifting poses irreparable consequences to chrono-integrity should the user fail to honor Coalition guidelines."

"I know the fucking rules! Just do it!"

"Initializing."

A final artillery shell was fired from the Man-O-War's canon just before the machine collapsed inward and buckled under its warped and melted frame. When the shell cleared the canon, time was dragged to a near stop, but not for Gideon, who was able to move at a normal rate.

Afflicted and exhausted, Gideon stumbled out of the impending blast zone. As he struggled through the grass field, he noticed that the stalks remained stiff and frozen as he disturbed them with his motion.

Several steps later, Gideon turned back to see the copper body of the artillery behaving the same way. The lethal explosive was crawling at a near standstill toward Gideon's prior position.

Just as he returned to the perimeter of the village, Gideon vanished without intent, teleporting out of time and to another realm.

.   .   .

When Gideon reappeared, it was not in the world he knew. He was standing in a vast barren desert bordered in all directions by a raging, swirling storm of infinite scale. The tempest's deep red walls were thousands of miles high and layered with unrelenting celestial disturbance. It was as if Gideon were standing in the eye of a hurricane made of birthing and dying cosmos. Though the center was less chaotic, the winds were still so violent that Gideon's body was pulled apart, but would strangely and miraculously reassemble.

Once Gideon was finally able to stand against the tumultuous winds, he lifted a section of his mask near his mouth and spat out a thick stream of blood. With forceful steps, he tried to move, but with each attempt he was pulled apart and reassembled at his point of origin in the realm. After several attempts, Gideon saw pieces of metal fly out from the walls of the storm. As the fragments emerged, they magnetized to a fixed point in the air, eventually forming and shaping what looked like a humanoid figure walking toward Gideon.

With a hostile posture, the mechanized humanoid approached Gideon, who was unable to run or move. Just as the machine reached out to grab him, Gideon was pulled into a million pieces and taken by the storm like sand in a tornado. As he was pulled apart, Gideon shouted and screamed until none of him remained.

.　　.　　.

When Gideon reappeared, it was on the dirt floor of the village. He was immobile, unconscious, and fuming with a thick vapor.

His sudden and strange appearance was witnessed by Arlo and the others, provoking them to leave cover and investigate.

"What the fuck?" asked Lambert to Arlo as they came together.

"I— I don't know. He didn't tell me what he was doing," said Arlo as he felt the incessant heat permeating from Gideon's body. "He's scorching."

"He said nothing?" asked Bohden.

"No. He just gave me his radio."

"This doesn't make sense. How did he take that entire thing down?" Lambert asked as he struggled to fathom what had happened.

"I don't know," replied Arlo as Lucy cautiously sniffed and paced Gideon's body, whimpering softly as she did.

"Well, our luck isn't gonna last. We need a way out of here," urged Lambert as he looked for options amongst the wreckage.

Struck with an idea, Arlo used Gideon's radio. He clicked the channel open and told the operator on the other end, "Liberty, this is two-five. Enemy armor has been neutralized, but we've lost Gideon."

"Understood, two-five. Imperial assets are still blocking our access to you. Are you able to reposition to the north?"

Before responding, Arlo looked at his team, who was barely left standing. "We will see what we can do." Arlo then ended the radio transmission.

"Are they out of their fucking minds? How are we supposed to move!? Gale can't even walk. Not to mention, what are we supposed to do with him?" Lambert said, referring to Gideon's motionless, steaming body.

"I don't know. But he's not dead . . . he's still breathing," replied Bohden, noticing Gideon's chest subtly rise and fall.

"Lovely," said Lambert.

The sudden sound of a wailing engine was heard from just beyond the wreckage of the village. A pickup truck then came sliding in from behind a mound of rubble.

Rounding the corner, the truck came to a dirt-filled, skidding halt just beside Arlo and the others. From the driver's door emerged Pearson in an urgent state.

Bohden was first to address the young maverick. "Pearson!?"

"I know, I know, I shouldn't be here, but they brought us to this field and then I heard what was happening over the radio. I told them I knew the way to you, but they wouldn't let me go, so I stole the truck and came."

"How did you steal a truck?" asked Arlo.

"Bohden taught me," Pearson said, prompting a look of confusion from Arlo to Bohden.

"Aye, chief, that's my fault. I did."

"You're mad, kid, but you've made a fan out of me. Well done," said Lambert as he walked toward the truck.

"Do you know a way north?" Arlo asked.

Pearson nodded and added, "I know these whole woods. I can get us out of here, at least back to their base."

Arlo then commanded the group accordingly. "Alright, everyone load up. Lambert, help me get Gideon onboard."

"How? He'll melt our hands if we touch him."

"Grab that metal panel. We'll use it as a stretcher."

Lambert ran to a large heap of rubble to recover a destroyed metal slab that was once part of a village gate. The ruptured metal was just wide enough to fit Gideon's body.

Once the slab was on the ground beside Gideon, Arlo wrapped his hands in as much loose clothing as he could. He grabbed Gideon and heaved him up. Even with fast, careful movements, the scalding temperature reached Arlo's hands and burned through the first layer of skin before he was finished moving Gideon.

"Fuck all!" said Arlo, wincing as he ripped the burnt fabric away.

While Arlo recovered, Pearson leaped in to help Lambert lift the improvised metal stretcher into the truck bed.

With Gideon's body secure, Bohden lifted Gale off the ground. As he endured the acute pain of moving, Gale ground his teeth and grunted with deep breaths to fight against the misery. Bohden loaded Gale into the passenger seat of the truck where his leg could remain stretched out.

Urgently, the rest of the team jumped into the truck bed, ready for Pearson to lead their escape deeper into the northern woods of the Neutral Zone.

.   .   .

Teenage adventure and wonder had given Pearson a vast knowledge of the local highways and roads, which he used to find an old back way that led into the open country.

As the beauty of the untainted rural view passed

by, Arlo could not help but think of the contrast. Were it any other day, or any other situation, such a moment could have been mistaken for an escape into a beautiful world devoid of the calamity he was drowning in. But all reprieves were once again cut short by the hounding pursuit of the Empire.

From beyond the trees, everyone heard the threat of swirling rotor blades. An attack helicopter then became visible as the truck came around the curved highway. Up the road, the aircraft was strategically positioned in a low hover, several feet above the asphalt. Pearson reacted by bringing the truck to a slow crawl.

As the wheels came to a stop, Arlo stood up to get a visual assessment. He could see that marksmen with rifles were seated on both sides of the chopper. A voice then came through from a loudspeaker. "Remain where you are, or you will be fired upon. All of you are under arrest."

A second helicopter then cut in from the other direction and quickly lowered itself to land in the road behind them.

Arlo's team was boxed in.

From the cabin of the helicopter, two mechanized

Imperial drones jumped out and approached the truck with their rifles aimed. Their gears and hydraulics spun and pressed with each step. In a cold machine voice, one of the units told everyone, "Place your hands on your head and remain where you are."

As the encroaching defeat began to suffocate their hopes, Arlo looked around for options, for anything. "It can't end like this," Arlo said under his breath as he watched Lambert discreetly drag his rifle back toward him with his feet.

In the truck cabin, Gale was looking ahead to the blocked road. With his systematic mind, he observed that the aircraft's hover was anything but steady. The winds were too high and were rocking the small, light frame back and forth. Even for him, it would be a tough shot to land, especially if Pearson accelerated off the road.

Gale then looked over his shoulder and saw Arlo with his hands on his head, the sight of which was enough to compel Gale to quietly propose, "On my mark, I want you to floor it forward and then take us into the forest."

Careful not to make any sudden movements, Pearson kept his eyes on the Imperials while he answered

Gale. "There's nothing but trees. How are we—?"

"Go. Now!" bellowed Gale.

Pearson slammed his foot into the gas pedal and the truck jumped forward. The jarring momentum caused Arlo and everyone in the back to fall to the bed floor. As the truck raced forward, several gunshots were fired from the helicopter in front, but they went astray, hitting the radiator and headlights.

Pearson cranked the wheel to the right and sent the truck off-road. The uneven ground shook the vehicle with violent tremors. Rocks and debris clanged against the metal undercarriage. Ahead, Pearson saw nothing but a wall of trees that he was on a collision course with. "Was this part of the plan?" he shouted.

"It's better than where we were headed! Shoot the gap!" replied Gale.

As soon as the truck passed through the space between the trees, the wheels began to slide and shift across the loose forest floor. Pearson then slammed on the brakes, attempting to regain control, but it was too late. All hope for correction was lost.

"Pull right! Pull right!" commanded Gale as he noticed they were about to crash into a massive pine.

Frantically, Pearson cranked and twisted the wheel, but nothing happened; the truck wheels were locked in place and gliding across the dirt like a runaway sled.

The first thing to impact the four-foot-wide tree trunk was the driver's side door. Pearson was tossed forward and then back. His head collided with the steering wheel and then backward into the head rest.

In the same moment of impact, Arlo and Gideon were thrown from the truck bed and onto the dirt. Gideon's armored frame had saved him from anything catastrophic. Arlo, however, hit with enough force to dislocate his shoulder. But even after, he kept rolling some distance forward and was torn apart by rocks and branches that impaled and punctured his body.

With the truck still sliding beyond control, Pearson realized that he could do nothing to steer the truck away from the impending second collision. With only seconds to decide, Gale unbuckled and yelled, "Bail out!"

Without hesitation, those who remained in the truck took their chances and leaped for the ground.

Pearson and Gale were first to hit, followed shortly after by Lambert and Bohden. Lucy was the only one able to make an agile and graceful leap to the ground, but even she tumbled several times before regaining herself.

As Gale rolled over from his crash landing, he saw the truck still in one piece before it smashed headfirst into a tree. He then turned to see that both Lambert and Bohden survived but were slow to recover. As he moved for his rifle, he was crippled by a new pain. He could feel that his fracture extended up into his hip.

When Lambert was finally able to stand, he saw that Arlo was struggling to get Gideon's body back on the stretcher. "Bohden! Get Gale! I'll help the others," yelled Lambert while running to Arlo.

With what little of his strength remained, Arlo lifted and dragged Gideon's metal stretcher across the dirt and back toward his body. Lambert criticized Arlo, telling him, "I can appreciate what you're doing, but we'll die trying to get him out of here."

"You heard him. We can't leave him for the Imperials. We can't just hand them this technology."

"Did you not see what they sent after us?"

"He can see the future. None of this makes sense unless that's true."

"We don't know that, Arlo."

"Maybe not you. But I know it."

Realizing that he was not going to break Arlo's stubborn will, Lambert did his best to improvise a solution. "Hopefully this armor is as good as it looks," Lambert said as he fastened a steel carabiner to a metal loop on the back side of Gideon's armor. He then ran a thick rope through the carabiner, creating a way to pull Gideon's body forward.

Both men heaving as hard as they were able, dragged Gideon's rigid body back to the crash site, only to discover the extent of Gale's injury.

"How bad is it?" asked Arlo between exhausted breaths.

"Not good," said Bohden. "The swelling has doubled, which means there's an internal bleed."

"If I stay here, I can hold off the first wave and keep 'em pinned. Might buy you guys some time," said Gale as he scooted himself to rest against a tree.

"No. You're coming with us. Pearson! Help lift him."

"Arlo, I know what I'm doing. My place is here now," Gale persisted with a calm, assuring voice.

Before Arlo could say more, the deep sound of Imperial helicopters shook everything nearby as several passed overhead and settled to a hover near the crash site.

"Go! Now!" demanded Gale before any more doubt could seize their time. Arlo and Lambert then gripped Gideon's rope-pull over their shoulders and dashed forward into the uneven forest terrain. Pearson and Lucy followed just behind. Bohden, however, remained in place, drawing a startled look from the others.

"Bohden! Let's go!" ordered Arlo.

"We'll be right behind you, chief," he replied.

Knowing there was no way to convince him otherwise, Arlo gathered the only words he could. "Good luck."

Bohden then told Pearson, who was the most stricken by the choice, "Stay strong, kid. I'll see you on the other side."

From the cabins of both Imperial helicopters, ropes were tossed out to deploy several squads of soldiers. One after the other, the Imperial reinforcements descended the long ropes and landed on the forest floor. By the time the choppers finished the deployment and broke off from their hover, they had dropped in no less than twenty fresh troopers.

Upon hearing the encroaching voices of the Imperial soldiers, Bohden lifted Gale and headed for the wreckage of the truck. As he carried Gale's tattered body, Gale did all he could to fight the excruciating pain of the movements. He winced and tensed, but nothing was enough to suppress the deep pain of fractured bones grinding in place.

Bohden eventually placed Gale into the driver's seat, providing him the extra cover of the thick steel truck frame. Before handing Gale his rifle, Bohden checked the magazine and then racked the feeder to load it up. The loud metal bolt sounded with a smashing *cling*.

"You're topped off and ready," said Bohden as Gale took the rifle.

"Where you gonna be?"

"Right beside you. Try to keep them from getting our flank." Bohden then took off his trauma vest and slung it over the driver's seat to give Gale an extra layer of ballistic protection.

"I can't take this. . . ." Gale contested as the vest was put in place.

"We're gonna make it out of here, both of us," Bohden replied as he secured the vest down.

Bohden then pulled himself away and moved to the passenger's side where he grabbed his machine gun. Weapon in hand, he lowered himself behind the truck frame and opened the gun's hatch cover, which allowed him to feed in a full belt of ammo.

As he pulled back the charging handle, Gale called out, "Here they come!"

Bohden stood up and slammed the gun on the truck bed wall. Instantly, he opened fire in small, barking bursts.

Countless zings, cracks, and hisses sounded all around the Imperials as the machine-gun fire came upon them, driving them to search for cover. As they were chased away, several among them were quickly gunned down by Gale's precision shots. "Scratch three!" boasted Gale.

"Keep it up!" Bohden replied, noticing his ammo belt was empty after firing the last few rounds. He shouted to Gale, "Reloading!"

"Copy. Covering!" said Gale in response. He then leaned up and fired several shots into the tree line.

Nothing connected, but it was enough to keep the Imperials back for a much-needed reprieve.

Before Gale could fire off another burst, he noticed that two more helicopters entered the area and were fast roping in another large squad of reinforcements. Even worse was that Gale could also see convoys of black trucks swarming in from the nearby road, many of which were filled with dozens more Imperial soldiers. "Shit," he said to himself.

.   .   .

In a grass field not far from the border of the Neutral Zone, an Imperial mobile command operation was rapidly assembled to handle the crisis the Empire was now facing from the intervention of Gideon's Coalition. As Imperial squadrons scrambled about the area, a troop transport helicopter came in for a rapid landing in the center of the field. Standing by to meet the aircraft was an intelligence officer overseeing operations in the area.

Once the helicopter settled, an afflicted Harper leaped out to take charge of the situation. The damage to her surface was such that her cybernetic interior was

CLARK RAYDER

exposed through numerous gashes and punctures. Her once-regal uniform was replaced by a loose black cowl that covered her like a robe.

Upon her arrival, Harper was approached by the intelligence officer, of whom she demanded, "What is the situation?"

"All our forces are in pursuit, ma'am, but several of our squadrons are under heavy fire from an entrenchment. They've requested an air strike."

"No. We will be phasing out human assets soon, anyway. I look forward to filling the vacancies. But instead of wasting my time with useless proposals, maybe find me someone who has an explanation for why the Americans now have an army."

"Nobody has been able to figure that out just yet, ma'am, but we are working on it," replied the officer, nearly whimpering, as he followed Harper's determined pace.

"Then task a non-human asset to solve it."

.   .   .

For Bohden and Gale, what began as a hopeful attempt to

hold off the Imperial advance was devolving into futility. Both men were losing track of just how fast the swarming Imperial horde was growing around them. All they could tell was that the return gunfire had evolved from stray blind shots and was now an unrelenting downpour of close calls and inevitable wounds. A nearly unbroken stream of bullets was tearing into the truck frame, causing sparks and debris to erupt like loose fireworks.

With his precision skill, Gale managed to keep up a kill count, but eventually, he fired his last two shots. He called to Bohden from the gun-smoke-filled cabin, "Loading!"

"Don't quit! We got this!" replied Bohden during a break in machine-gun fire. As best he could manage, Gale ejected the rifle magazine and quickly searched his vest for a fully loaded one. As he reached for his pouches, gunshots cracked through the windshield and the dash, provoking him to lean down even farther as he struggled to reload.

Without Gale's help, the volume of fire kept increasing. Bohden knew he had to break up the assault. He took a deep breath and rose again to fire. As he did, a round tore into his left shoulder, and then another into his forearm. A cloud of red mist blew out from both hits and his body was then speckled red. Bohden, however, did not let go of the trigger, he kept it pressed until the belt ran dry. He yelled to Gale in a shaken voice, "I'm out! Cover!"

Luckily, Gale was now ready to reengage. He managed to feed a new magazine and release the bolt. "I got it!" Gale said as he leaned up and aimed into the woods. He fired one, two, and finally a third shot. Each round found a target and dropped them to the ground, but nothing seemed to be enough to break up the constant incoming fire from the Imperials.

One round and then another finally hit Gale from an Imperial team flanking to the side. The first shot went into his leg, the other into his shoulder. As blood sprayed across the cabin, Gale groaned, "I'm hit!" He then fired off a whole sequence of stray shots out of the driver's side window, hoping it would give him a moment to recover.

Outside, Bohden was struggling with his able arm to load his final ammo belt. The heat from the gun was scorching, and without another hand to hold the weapon, he realized he could not reload before losing Gale. He ditched the machine gun and grabbed his backpack.

After tossing open the flap, he grabbed one of a dozen explosive charges that he found among Ezra's supply. Rapidly, Bohden shoved the metallic receiver into the soft clay-like charge. He then grabbed the detonator from the pocket and concealed it in his hand. With his other hand, Bohden drew his sidearm and readied himself to grab Gale from the cabin.

As he stood up, two Imperials converged from the trees. When they fell within range, Bohden fired and took one down, but then shots came from the distance and punctured his right shoulder.

Collapsing to the ground, Bohden had enough strength left in him to inch his way back toward the truck cabin. He fought his crippled limbs to reload his pistol. His hand tremored and shook from his wounds as he tried to place the magazine in. But as he heard boots approaching, he winced past the pain and jammed the magazine in. Just as the first bullet chambered, an Imperial emerged around the corner, provoking Bohden to fire everything he had left. Beneath the eruptions of blood, the converging soldier fell backwards, lifeless before hitting the dirt.

Bohden was afforded no reprieve, for as soon as the Imperial fell, two more rushed to take his place. As they swarmed closer, Bohden could do nothing but pull on a dry trigger that clicked and clicked. Bohden tossed the pistol at them before they could fire, disrupting them for long enough for Gale to fire and kill them both.

Bewildered, Bohden looked back to see Gale fall out of the truck cabin and onto the dirt floor, his clothes and gear soaked in blood. Desperate to keep hope alive, Bohden rolled over and rose from the ground. He reached to grab a rifle from the Imperial corpse closest to him. Giving it to Gale, Bohden told him, "I'm gonna get us behind the trees. Cover me!"

Bohden shook off the crippling pain of all his wounds and yanked the back of Gale's vest to drag him away from the truck. Gale had no more than ten rounds left in the rifle, which he quickly spent on the few Imperials in range. Before he could fire his last shot, both he and Bohden heard the terrible sound of the forest being torn down by approaching Imperial armor.

Up ahead, they saw three armored troop carriers crawling toward them. Whole trees were torn down and trampled by the vehicle's goliathan power.

"Gotta give 'em credit for persistence," mumbled Bohden.

Gale realized his blood loss had reached a critical point. He said to Bohden in a fading breath, "It's been an honor. . . ."

"Don't give up on me, Gale! Not now!" said Bohden as they came around the cover of a thick pine. Setting Gale against the bark, Bohden looked to see that Gale's eyes were frozen.

He was gone.

Bohden's eyes watered at the sight of Gale's hollow face. He looked to the detonator in his hand. Before pressing the trigger, Bohden let out a bellowing war cry that thundered across the fight.

.   .   .

The sound of the explosion carried over a mile to where it fell upon the remainder of Arlo's team. The alarming disturbance prompted them to a halt.

"The hell was that?" Lambert asked with gasping breaths from the arduous run. Arlo shook his head. "I don't know. . . ."

The group then heard the crackling static of a transmission coming through Gideon's radio. A voice followed just after, saying, "Two-five, this is Liberty. We have reestablished our ISR feed and are tracking you now, but we need to know what your status is on the ground. Are you able to shift course to the east?"

Urgently, Arlo grabbed the radio and opened a channel. "Only if you see something we don't."

"Less than a klick to the east, the forest turns to an open pasture. That's the best option for us to land a casevac team with close air support. But I need to know, are you able to make the distance?"

Arlo briefly looked to Lambert and Pearson, who both gave Arlo an assuring nod. Arlo nodded back and told the Coalition operator, "We'll be there."

"Bloody 'ell!" said Lambert as he readied himself and gripped the pull cable with his blistered hands.

Revived with the hope of rescue, the group rallied and began the long sprint to the extraction zone. Lucy led the way, carving the best path through the unlevel terrain that went on for some distance until eventually she encountered a large slope that led out of the forest.

With agile leaps, she vaulted up a small set of

rocks that allowed her to climb to the top, where she immediately began barking at the sight of the Imperial forces closing in.

Coming to the base of the hill, Arlo and Lambert searched around for another option, but harsh vertical drop-offs extended out on both sides of the slope.

"How are we supposed to drag him up this?" asked Pearson at the sight of the intimidating hillside.

Urged to hasten the climb, Lambert rushed forward and scaled the first set of rocks. Once he was halfway up the hill, he dragged Gideon's body to the base and held the rope, waiting for the next man to climb. "We can do it. Come on," he grunted, fighting the pain of his bursting blisters, which were finally torn apart by the rope.

"Go! Go!" said Arlo, who pressed Pearson forward to climb.

With his youthful resilience, Pearson rapidly made it to Lambert and took the rope from his blood-soaked hands. As Pearson and Lambert heaved Gideon's body up, zipping whistles of gunfire fell upon the hillside.

Lambert urgently slung his rifle forward and

opened fire into the trees with several quick bursts, but before he could continue the assault, he noticed that Pearson was not strong enough to get Gideon past the summit of the hill. "Just hold on," he said to Pearson as he slid down the hill to grab Arlo's hand and pull him up.

Once past the rocks, Arlo clawed the dirt to pull himself to Pearson and take the rope. The boy let go, then Lambert handed over his rifle and said, "You can shoot, right!? Keep 'em pinned!"

Pearson nodded, then shouldered the rifle, firing off round after round toward the Imperials as Arlo and Lambert made the final climb to the hilltop, dragging Gideon's body the final thirty yards.

Just as Arlo cleared the last of the slope, he turned on his back, armed himself with this rile and shouted, "Covering fire! Move up! Move up!"

Pearson broke off his attack and dashed up the hill. Parallel to him, Arlo unleashed a volley of suppressing fire, enough to allow Pearson to scale the hill and reach the others.

"Let's go! Let's go!" shouted Arlo as he and Lambert once again picked up the rope and sprinted forward. "That's them! I can hear it!" Arlo continued as he heard the echo of a helicopter engine.

Just beyond the top of the hill, the open field could finally be seen through the forest. All that remained was closing the short distance.

"I see smoke!" said Lambert at the sight of a bright red haze carried by the wind toward the team.

Crossing nearly halfway, an Imperial grenade fired from a launcher at the base of the hill hit a tree behind Pearson, the force of which blew him to the ground and engulfed him in an eruption of debris and dirt. Arlo dashed back and pulled Pearson up. As the layers of dirt spilled off him, he could see that the young boy was confused and disoriented from the concussive force. "You're gonna be fine! Come on!" Arlo said as he rushed Pearson to press forward.

When the group crossed the threshold of the forest, they entered a massive, abandoned farm field that stretched out for several miles. Waiting near the tree line was an idling heavy helicopter with the back ramp lowered, awaiting Arlo's team. Surrounding it were several active smoke grenades spewing red exhaust to mark their position.

Arlo and Lambert finally collapsed from the

crippling exhaustion that had burned out every fiber of muscle.

"Fuck all!" blared Lambert as he fought to recover and stand on wobbly, buckling legs.

"Come on! We can make it!" shouted Arlo with nearly nothing left in his lungs but wheezing gasps.

"I can't fuckin' do it, Arlo! I can't stan—" said Lambert as his knees collapsed.

Arlo doubled back and lifted Lambert over his shoulder, gripping the cable in his hand as he did. "Come on! Come on!" he said as he heaved and lifted the nearly dead weight of Lambert's body.

To hasten the evacuation, a team of five Coalition soldiers leaped from the helicopter cabin and sprinted to Arlo's team. Two men took Lambert from Arlo, and another two took over pulling Gideon's body across the grass.

A wave of whistling gunfire then ripped past the team, sending them into the weeds for cover.

"Fuck!" Arlo shouted as he rolled over and fired several rounds into the tree line with his rifle. The Coalition soldiers did the same, unloading waves of suppressing fire that interrupted the Imperial assault.

"Move! Move!" the Coalition team shouted as they recovered and resumed their retreat to the helicopter amidst the break in the gunfire.

As they crossed the field, another transmission came through the radio. This time it was a nearby pilot informing the team, "All friendlies, all friendlies, this is Skyknight. We are en route to provide close air support. Be advised, we will be engaging hostiles to your south and southeast. Tally to target, ten seconds."

"Copy that Skyknight!" shouted the lead Coalition soldier into his radio. He then turned to address everyone, saying, "Get ready! Danger close!"

Not a moment after the transmission ended, an Imperial armored vehicle crushed through the tree line and fired several deep, booming artillery shells that whistled past the extraction helicopter. As the vehicle adjusted for a follow-up attack, a large swarm of Imperial foot soldiers followed behind. The soldiers immediately fell into formation behind the cover of the Imperial armor as it dragged forward through the field.

"Contact left!" shouted the Coalition soldiers.

The pressure of a sonic crack sounded and shook the field. A flight of two Coalition jets then appeared over the tree line. As the low-flying fighters roared toward the Imperial forces, numerous air-to-ground missiles ignited and fired from the wings of both aircraft.

Tearing across the field, the missiles hit, impacting with nothing short of colossal force. Each came one after the other in a domino-like sequence that rocked the ground with tectonic pulses. Following less than a second behind the missile strike was the deep, blaring sound of heavy Gatling gunfire that echoed throughout the field.

The jets zoomed out of the area and cracked the sky with sonic reverberations. Arlo turned back to see that the strike had incinerated everything in its path. Nothing remained but scorched earth and twisted metal wreckage.

The Coalition leader urged the team to press on, shouting, "We gotta move! More are coming!"

Arlo stumbled forward, grabbing Pearson along the way, and sprinted for the helicopter with all he had left.

He finally reached the ramp of the Coalition chopper. He lifted Pearson inside and then collapsed onto the metal floor. Lambert was beside him, heaving and gasping for air while clutching Lucy with his arm.

"That's it! That's everyone! Let's go! Let's go!" came a voice from the Coalition squadron. After being given the order to finally load in, one by one they all pulled away from the fight and secured themselves in the cabin.

Arlo watched as the helicopter lifted from the field and turned to the north. Once airborne, his eyes looked to the tree line, where he could see several more Imperial armored vehicles had breached through with dozens more foot soldiers following behind them.

The threat, however, was answered by a second set of fighters that roared through the area and unleashed another wave of devastating air strikes. At the sight of the field being detonated, Arlo rested his head against the metal floor and closed his eyes.

EPILOGUE

Once more, a devoted sun had risen. Barely veiled by a thin cloud cover, the light of the new day graced a vast tundra terrain.

The Coalition helicopters extracted what remained of Arlo's team almost eight hundred miles north, where at the base of a humble, moss-covered mountain there was a colossal concrete bunker carved into the rock. It was the ideal realm for Gideon's enigmatic Coalition.

As the helicopters made their final approach toward an ice-crusted helipad, Arlo grabbed the cabin frame and leaned out against the windchill to better glimpse the new surroundings. For miles the terrain was dark green grass filled with jagged rocks and hills. Sparse, flat lakes filled the rest of the view with their unmoving waters. In the far distance, snow-topped mountains enclosed the horizon, touching all the way to a dreary, frozen sky.

Arlo turned his eyes to the bunker. The opening was a colossal rectangular mouth with monolithic blast doors left open for the team's arrival. In front of the bunker were all the makings of a standard military operation: personnel, equipment, antennae, and generators to keep everything powered.

The landing winds of the helicopter blew the loose snow into a focused blizzard. The small team of Coalition operatives that arrived to meet the aircraft stood unaffected amidst the breezy tumult.

As soon as the helicopter settled, the landing team rushed to retrieve Gideon's body. With them was a hovering gurney that they pushed through the air and rested near the idling aircraft.

Traveling through the night, Gideon's body had cooled to a manageable level that Arlo and Lambert were able to handle. After setting him upon the gurney, an operative spoke to Arlo. "Thank you for saving him."

"Is he gonna make it?" asked Arlo.

"We will do our best," replied the operative, who then took Gideon away and into the bunker.

Arlo and Lambert moved to witness the second

aircraft land, allowing Troy to set foot onto the strange new frontier. Troy stepped out of the aircraft with Eliza, placed her down, then guided her by the hand to Pearson.

As the siblings reunited, Arlo and Lambert were approached by a man who emerged from the bunker. When the figure crossed through the swirling snow and ice, his rugged Arctic attire became visible to Arlo. "Welcome to the tundra. Name's Declan West. Coalition Intelligence. Nice to finally meet you."

"Your voice . . . Was that you on the radio?"

"It was. You guys sure went through hell. I'm sorry for the others who didn't make it."

"Have you confirmed that?" asked Lambert.

"Last we saw of them was an explosion on the ISR feed. I will say, whatever they did, it bought you all enough time to get out."

Overwhelmed, Arlo looked to the horizon, shaking his head in disbelief.

Lambert then placed his hand on Arlo's shoulder. "They went out on their terms, Arlo."

"Is this where all of you have been this whole time?" Arlo suggested, attempting to distract himself.

"I'm afraid it's not that simple, but come inside.

The sooner we get started the better."

Once inside the bunker doors, Declan led everyone through the main hangar of the compound, which was a monument to military engineering. Hundreds of feet spanned from rock wall to rock wall, all of which was bolstered with heavy steel frames secured into the granite interior. The area itself was filled with dozens of aircraft, fighter jets, bombers, and helicopters, many of which were attended by Coalition maintenance crews and personnel.

Not long after Arlo's team entered the bunker, a single Coalition fighter made a roaring approach and then landed on the frozen runway. Once the aircraft settled into its landing, it taxied to the blast doors where it was met by a small band of flight ops personnel.

"I had a whole squadron of them sent out to keep the Imperials from following your flight in," said Declan at the sight of the lone aircraft. "Hopefully more return soon."

"How long have you been here?" wondered Lambert as he studied the depth of the clandestine base.

"Time has a different meaning around here. But to answer your question, we set up not long after the outbreak of the war. I'm sure Gideon mentioned that we've been observing things from afar to determine if our intervention was necessary."

"A lot more people could be alive right now if you had reached that decision sooner," said Arlo.

"Not necessarily, no. But I understand how it can appear that way. Give me a chance to explain why and then maybe you'll see things differently," said Declan, who came to a stop near a control console. He glanced up to Arlo and Lambert, telling them, "I'm sorry, but where we're heading is no place for children. They will have to wait up here."

Troy nodded and told everyone, "I'll find a spot for us to wait."

After Troy led Pearson and Eliza away, Declan told Arlo and Lambert, "Before we head down, it's my obligation to advise you that if you proceed, you agree to hear and witness information that will forever change your understanding of the world."

"You're not one for small talk, are you," Lambert said.

"Is that a yes?"

"We've made it this far. No sense in going back

now," replied Arlo.

Declan nodded and pressed a large industrial button on the console beside him.

The air was filled with echoing booms of levers and machines that moved the hollow floor and revealed it to be a cargo lift. The massive fifty-foot by fifty-foot platform pulled away from ground level and began descending into the depths of the mountain.

If you enjoyed The Liberty Wars, please consider leaving your honest review on Amazon.